Just Shy
of Harmony

Also by Philip Gulley
in Large Print:

Home to Harmony

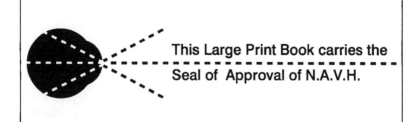

This Large Print Book carries the
Seal of Approval of N.A.V.H.

Just Shy
of Harmony

Philip Gulley

Thorndike Press • Waterville, Maine

Published in 2002 by arrangement with
HarperCollins Publishers, Inc.

Thorndike Press Large Print Americana Series.

The tree indicium is a trademark of Thorndike Press.

The text of this Large Print edition is unabridged.
Other aspects of the book may vary from the original edition.

Set in 16 pt. Plantin by Al Chase.

Printed in the United States on permanent paper.

Library of Congress Cataloging-in-Publication Data
Gulley, Philip.
    Just shy of Harmony / Philip Gulley.
        p. cm.
    ISBN 0-7862-4514-X (lg. print : hc : alk. paper)
    1. Clergy — Fiction.   2. Quakers — Fiction.   3. Indiana
— Fiction.   4. City and town life — Fiction.   5. Large type
books.   I. Title.
PS3557.U449 J87 2002b
    813´.54—dc21   2002028608

To Joan and my sons, Spencer and Sam

Acknowledgments

I am indebted to the good people at HarperSanFrancisco for valuing truth above conformity. Their open minds and gracious hearts are deep refreshment.

Contents

Acknowledgments		6
1. *Just Shy of Harmony*		9
2. *Dale's Dream*		23
3. *When a Man Loves a Woman*		35
4. *Sam's Fading Faith*		47
5. *Hard Times*		57
6. *The Legacy*		68
7. *The Date*		79
8. *The Jackpot*		91
9. *A Dubious Blessing*		105
10. *A Hint of Hope*		120
11. *Jessie and Asa Come to Terms*		134
12. *No More Wing Buds*		147
13. *A Sweet Liberation*		158
14. *On the Night of Love Reborn*		170
15. *A Beautiful Week*		181
16. *Peace on Earth*		192
17. *A Winter Blessing*		204
18. *A Ministry of Availability*		215
19. *Refreshed*		227
20. *The Smallest Good*		239
21. *The Caribbean*		252
22. *Bea and the Reverend*		264
23. *The Ministry of Noodles*		275

24. *A Time to Die* 287
25. *A Reason to Hope* 301
26. *The Hour of Truth* 308

One

Just Shy of Harmony

Sam Gardner sat on the porch the Monday after Easter. It was early in the morning. The Grant kids were walking past on their way to school.

"Are Levi and Addison ready?" Billy Grant yelled from the sidewalk.

"They'll be right out," Sam answered.

The window by the porch swing was propped open. Sam could hear his wife, Barbara, giving their boys last-minute instructions.

"Levi, don't forget your lunch money. Addison, if you have to go pee-pee, tell the teacher. Please don't go in your pants. Just raise your hand and ask to use the bathroom. Can you do that, honey?"

The boys walked out the front door with their mother following behind, adjusting their shirt collars and smoothing their hair. "Behave yourselves. Obey your teachers."

Barbara settled herself on the porch swing next to Sam. She let out a heavy sigh.

"Addison's kindergarten teacher called

9

yesterday. Do you know he's wet his pants twice in the past week?"

"He is an unusually moist child," Sam agreed.

A pickup truck rattled past their house. Ellis and Miriam Hodge driving Amanda to school. Ellis bumped the truck horn.

"There go the Hodges," Sam observed.

"I really like them," Barbara said.

"I wish we had ten more just like them."

They swung back and forth in a companionable silence.

"I was looking at the calendar," Barbara said. "I had forgotten this Sunday is Goal-Setting Sunday."

Sam groaned. "Oh, that's right. I'd forgotten too. I don't think I'll go."

"You have to go. You're the pastor."

"Maybe I'll get lucky and die before then."

But the Lord didn't see fit to spare him. Instead, Goal-Setting Sunday gnawed at Sam the entire week.

That Thursday he read the "Twenty-five Years Ago This Week" column in the *Harmony Herald*. There was a mention of Dale Hinshaw's long-ago mission trip. Twenty-five years ago, one of their goals had been the development of "Lawn Mower Evangelism." Compelled by the Almighty, Dale had ridden across the state on his John Deere lawn tractor. Whenever he passed someone in their yard, Dale would give them a Bible tract and witness to them.

"We just have to throw the seed out there," Dale had told the *Herald.* "There's no telling what the Lord can do with it." Then he was quoted as saying, "Near as I can figure, I averaged eight miles to the gallon."

This Sunday promised to be another glorious chapter in the goal-setting history of Harmony Friends Meeting.

The first Goal-Setting Sunday was held in 1970, the year Pastor Taylor came to Harmony fresh from seminary, chock-full of grand ideas. Sam was nine years old and has a vague recollection of Pastor Taylor standing at the chalkboard in the meetinghouse basement, encouraging them to splendid heights.

In 1970, their goals were, one, to spread the gospel to every tribe and person in the world, two, to end world hunger, and, three, to carpet the Sunday school rooms.

They'd carpeted the Sunday school rooms first, donated a box of canned goods to a food pantry, and then lost their enthusiasm to do anything more.

Goal-Setting Sunday had gone downhill from there, each year a stark testimony to the growing apathy of the church.

At the last Goal-Setting Sunday, Dale Hinshaw had proposed painting *Jesus Saves* on the meetinghouse roof as a witness to people in airplanes. "They're up there in the wild blue yonder, bucking up and down in the turbulence. The pilot's telling them to fasten their seat belts. They'll look out the window and see our roof, and it'll fix their minds on the eternal. If they're not open to the Lord then, they never will be."

That was when Sam had proposed doing away with Goal-Setting Sunday. "Why do we even bother? We set these goals and make a big deal out of it for a month or so, then we forget all about it. When we do remember it, we feel bad that we didn't do anything. Why don't we just skip Goal-Setting Sunday this year?"

That had gone over like a pregnant pole-vaulter.

Dale had quoted from the book of Revelation about lukewarm churches and how God would spew them out of his mouth. "Do you want the Lord to spit us out, Sam? Is that what you want? 'Cause I tell you right now, that's what He'll do. You're leading us down a slippery slope. First, we'll stop doing the Goal-Setting Sunday, then the next thing you know there'll be fornication right here in the church. You watch and see."

Any deviation from tradition had Dale Hinshaw prophesying an outbreak of fornication in the church pews. It took Sam several years to learn he was better off keeping quiet and not suggesting anything new.

"Just go along with it," his wife had told him. "It's only one Sunday a year. Let them do whatever they're going to do. It's easier that way."

So when Dale suggested at the elders meeting that it was time for Goal-Setting Sunday, Sam didn't argue.

They scheduled it for the first Sunday after Easter, which is when they've always held it, lest fornication break out in the church.

Dale came to the meetinghouse on Goal-Setting Sunday clutching a briefcase. An ominous sign. After worship, everyone clumped downstairs. Miriam Hodge, the last bastion of sanity in the congregation and, providentially, the head elder, stood at the blackboard, chalk in hand. She asked Sam to pray, so he used the opportunity to

13

talk about the importance of tasteful ministry.

"Dear God," Sam prayed, "may whatever we do bring honor to your name. Let our ministry be proper and reverent, befitting your magnificence."

He'd no sooner said "Amen" than Dale jumped to his feet. "I've been giving this some thought and I've come up with some fine ideas."

He pulled a sheaf of papers from his briefcase and began reading an article from *Ripley's Believe It or Not* about a chicken who had swallowed a scrap of paper from a phone book, only to lay an egg with the name and phone number perfectly preserved in the yolk.

"And the amazing thing was, the man who cracked open the egg phoned the number on the scrap of paper. It was a lady in Illinois. He went to meet her and they ended up getting married. Now if that ain't the Lord working, I don't know what is," Dale said.

He suggested feeding chickens Bible passages and passing out the resultant Scripture eggs to unbelievers.

"There's no telling how the Lord could use that. I tell you right now, if I cracked open an egg and read that the wages of sin was death, I'd straighten up right quick."

Miriam Hodge thanked Dale for his idea. She wrote *Scripture eggs* on the blackboard.

"Dale, you've certainly given us something to think about. Does anyone else have any ideas?" Miriam asked.

Bill Muldock raised his hand. Bill was coach of the church softball team and had been wanting to expand into basketball.

"Well, here's my idea," Bill said. "I was thinking maybe we could start a basketball evangelism program. Maybe start a church basketball league. We could call it Heavenly Hoops. You know what they say in the Bible, 'All work and no play makes Johnny a dull boy.' At least, I think it says that in the Bible."

People began to argue about whether it said that in the Bible.

"Enough of this nonsense," Fern Hampton interrupted. "What this church needs is a vanity table in the women's rest room."

Sam sat in his folding chair, thinking of churches that had homeless shelters and soup kitchens and raised money to send doctors to Africa to help lepers. He wished there was a leper in Harmony they could help. There's nothing like a leper to stir up a church, he thought.

He was lost in the reverie of disease when Miriam Hodge spoke. "I read in the *Herald* last week that the mental-health center is trying to raise money. I thought we could hold a fund-raiser and help with that." She turned to Sam. "What do you think, Sam?"

Sam looked at Dale Hinshaw sitting in his chair, poring over his sheaf of papers.

"I suspect there are several people in this town who could benefit from therapy," Sam told her.

Dale Hinshaw rose to his feet. "I don't want to be a wet blanket, but the Lord won't let me keep quiet on this one. That mental-health group is a dangerous bunch, if you ask me. I think some of 'em might even be homosexual. At least they look that way to me. I just don't think we oughta be giving the Lord's money to the work of the devil."

"Well, I think helping the mental-health center is a wonderful idea," Jessie Peacock said.

Miriam wrote *mental health center* on the blackboard.

There were other ideas too discouraging to mention. They finally settled on three: Scripture eggs, a vanity for the women's rest room, and starting a Heavenly Hoops church basketball league.

Sam went home disheartened.

After Sunday dinner, the Gardners' phone rang. It was Fern Hampton, saying she wanted to be the one to choose the vanity. It made Sam tired, talking with her. He leaned against the kitchen cabinets as she spoke.

"Yeah, sure, Fern. Whatever," he said, and hung up the phone.

That evening he and Barbara put their boys to bed, then sat on the porch swing in the warm spring air. Barbara reached over and took his hand.

"What's wrong, honey?" she asked. "You're being awful quiet. Is something wrong?"

He sighed. "I'm not sure how much longer I can take this. Children are starving to death, and Bill Muldock wants to start a church basketball league." He snorted. "Heavenly Hoops. For crying out loud."

"It was like this last year, honey. Remember how tired you were after last year's Goal-Setting Sunday? Maybe you just need to take a few days off."

"I don't know. Every time I do that, I get all rested up, then go back to church and get discouraged all over again."

"Maybe talking with the other pastors in town would help," Barbara suggested.

Sam thought for a moment.

"No, I don't think so. The Baptist minister just quotes from the Psalms and the Catholic priest is practically deaf. You can't even talk with him."

"How about the minister at that new church? He seems like a nice enough guy."

"Pastor Jimmy at the Harmony Worship Center? You've got to be kidding. All he does is rub my nose in it." Sam mimicked the pastor. " 'Two hundred and sixty-two folks at church this week! A new record! The Lord is really blessing us. How's your church growing, Sam?'

"He knows we're not growing. How could we be? Half our members are going to his church. It's all a game to him. Last week he preached a sermon called 'Ten Mutual Funds Jesus Would Die For.' What on earth is the church coming to? I might as well be selling cars for Harvey Muldock for all the good it does. I don't know, maybe I shouldn't have become a pastor in the first place."

Sam had been thinking of quitting the ministry, but wasn't sure it was allowed. Being a pastor was like a life sentence with no parole. The year before, at the Quaker ministers' conference, he'd stayed up late one night and talked with another minister

18

about how frustrated he was.

"Yeah, I used to get that way," the other minister said. "Then I learned the secret of lasting in the pastoral ministry."

"What's that?" Sam asked.

"You got to stop caring. If you care about what happens in the church and what other people do, it'll break your heart every time. Put in your office hours, preach your sermons, make your hospital visits, go to the meetings, but don't get all wrapped up in it."

Sam frowned. "I don't know. That sounds pretty cynical."

"Cynicism is just another word for realism," the pastor said. He looked at Sam. "I know your type. You probably expect people in your church to act like Christians, don't you?"

"Well, yes, I guess I do."

"There's your problem, right there. Don't expect anything. That way, when they blow it, you're not caught off guard, and if they get something right, it's a pleasant surprise. See what I mean?"

"I'm not sure I can do that."

"I tell you, Sam, it's the only way to go. You don't expect anything from them, and after a while they won't expect anything from you, and everybody's happy. Oh, one or two of them will want something more, but if you're lucky, they won't stick around."

Sometimes Sam wondered if coming back to his hometown church had been a mistake. A big church in North Carolina had written last year to see if he wanted to be their pastor. He had thought about it for a few days, then turned them down. Now he wishes he'd given it more thought. Maybe that church would have been different.

The next week during the elders meeting, after he proposed an idea, Fern Hampton looked at him sideways and said, "Sam, why aren't you ever happy with the way things are? Your parents aren't like that. They don't go around agitating for change and getting folks all stirred up. Why are you always after us to try something new? Don't you like us the way we are?"

Sam explained it was his responsibility to encourage the congregation to grow in their faith.

"If we want to grow in our faith, we'll let you know," she said. "Otherwise, maybe you should just keep your opinion to yourself."

He wished he'd kept the letter from North Carolina.

Fern had apologized later, kind of.

"Maybe I shouldn't have said it quite like that, but I just don't think you oughta rush in here and make all these changes."

"Fern, I've been a member of this church most of my life, and the only thing I proposed was moving the pencil sharpener so the office door doesn't bang into it."

"My father put that pencil sharpener there, and he must have had a good reason." She began to weep, thinking of her father. "Now you've gotten me all upset again. See, that's just what I was talking about. You start in with your agitating, and now I'm all upset again. Why do you treat me this way?"

Sam had gone home and called the church in North Carolina, but by then they'd found a new pastor.

It was probably for the best. He'd have gone there, and for the first year everything would have been fine and they'd all have been happy. Then he'd have suggested a change, maybe starting a new Sunday school class or moving the pencil sharpener, and there'd have been wailing and gnashing of teeth. Probably better to stick with the devil he knew. Besides, his parents lived here, his kids liked their school, and Miriam and Ellis Hodge were supportive.

Maybe the other minister was right. Maybe it was better not to expect much.

That way, if folks accidentally acted like Christians, it would be a nice surprise, and if they didn't, he wouldn't be let down. Maybe the answer was instead of caring so much, he shouldn't care at all. In the meantime, there were plenty of other things to do. Bathroom vanities to install and basketball leagues to start.

After all, just because you've given up being the church doesn't mean life stops. There are committee meetings to attend and paperwork to fill out and a newsletter article to write inviting all interested men to blow the dust off their sneakers and come out for the new Heavenly Hoops basketball team. First practice, this Wednesday evening, at the school gym.

Two

Dale's Dream

Dale Hinshaw couldn't remember when he'd been so excited. Ever since he'd read the *Ripley's Believe It or Not* story, he'd been dreaming of the possibilities. Now, after several years of lobbying, he had finally persuaded the Harmony Friends Meeting to try Scripture eggs for one of their goals. He was beside himself. That night, Dale and his wife stayed up late, sitting in their recliners, too excited to sleep.

"You know, this could be big," Dale said. "This could be bigger than those 'What Did Jesus Do?' bracelets. Just think, unbelievers all over the country cracking open eggs for breakfast and having the Word right there, first thing in the morning. I think the Lord could really use this."

"It humbles me to think how God might use us," Dale's wife agreed.

They sat quietly in their recliners, awed by the glory of it.

"I'm not meaning to be vain," Dale said, "but I think I should be in charge of the Scripture egg project. I think the Lord has laid this on my heart. Maybe I ought to call Sam and tell him I want to be in charge."

"It's nearly midnight. Don't you think you should wait until morning?"

"Naw, this can't wait. Besides, he's a minister. He's used to getting phone calls late at night."

Dale released the catch on the chair, rose up from his recliner, and walked to the phone in the kitchen to dial Sam's number.

Sam answered on the eighth ring.

"Sam, this is Dale. Say, I've been thinking about our Scripture egg project. I want to be in charge. I believe the Lord's laid this on my heart."

They talked for a while, then Dale hung up the phone and walked back into the living room to sit down.

"Boy, that Sam sure is cranky," Dale told his wife. "Have you noticed that lately? He nearly bit my head off. If you ask me, he was downright rude."

"Well, honey, it just goes to show that not everyone has a servant's heart like you do."

Dale nodded. "I've always tried to be of service."

"That's what I love about you."

Dale and his wife had been married nearly

forty years. They met at the Ozark School of the Scriptures in 1958, where he'd taken classes on how to be a pastor and she'd studied how to be a pastor's wife. After school they married and Dale took a church, but it didn't work out, so he quit.

They moved to Harmony, where Dale began selling insurance and Mrs. Dale Hinshaw joined the Friendly Women's Circle. Not many people know her real name, which is Dolores. When she married, she folded her personality into Dale's and became Mrs. Dale Hinshaw. That's how she introduces herself. They raised three sons — Raymond Dale, Harold Dale, and Robert Dale. When the boys were little, the Hinshaws went to Mount Rushmore one summer. Five years ago, Dale bought a bass boat. Living the dream. But now Dale is thinking of retiring. His customers are dying off, and he hasn't been able to replace them.

He sits in his wood-paneled office at his green metal desk, underneath the Farmer's Mutual Insurance calendar, waiting for the door to swing open and the bell to tinkle. But the bell isn't tinkling much these days. He suspects people are buying their insurance off the Internet. He sees commercials on television about

Internet insurance companies.

"Will you look at that," he says to his wife. "You think if a tornado knocks your house down, those Silicone Valley people will come see you? You think they'll sponsor a Little League team? You think they'll send you a windshield scraper? You think they'll come visit you in the hospital when you're sick and dying? Not a chance."

Dale visits all his customers who are in the hospital. It's almost like being a pastor. He sits in a chair beside their bed and reads from the Bible about the Father's house having many mansions. Even if the people aren't dying. Even if they're just there to have their tonsils removed. He told his wife, "There's something about lying in a hospital bed that turns your mind toward the eternal."

Dale has never told anyone in Harmony that he had been a pastor. He and his wife have never talked about it. He feels guilty and ashamed. He feels he let the Lord down, that he gave up too quickly. He fears God is angry with him. But when he visits his customers in the hospital, the guilt eases and he feels at peace, as if he's doing what he was meant to do.

I should've stuck with the ministry, he tells himself.

He thinks about retiring from the insurance business and going back in the ministry. On Sunday mornings, he sits in his pew and listens to Sam preach and thinks, I could do better. All I need is the chance to prove myself.

He believes the Scripture egg project is that chance, that it's God's way of opening a door for him.

The week following Goal-Setting Sunday, Dale and his wife spent their evenings sitting at the kitchen table writing out Scripture verses on tiny slips of paper.

Dale thumbed through his Bible, looking for short verses that could be easily digested.

They wrote lots of *Jesus wept* verses. And *The wages of sin is death.* If he printed especially small, he could fit *This is the day the Lord has made, I will rejoice and be glad in it* onto the little slip. That was Dale's favorite verse of all. He imagined unbelievers finding that verse in their morning egg, having their hearts stirred, and coming to the Lord.

The hardest part, Dale surmised, would be getting the chickens to eat the slips of paper. After that, it was all downhill.

He talked about it with Asa Peacock

down at the Coffee Cup Restaurant one morning in early May. Asa raised chickens and was an expert on all matters fowl, but he'd never heard of anyone finding a piece of paper in an egg yolk.

"Oddest thing I ever heard," Asa said. "You say you read about it in *Ripley's Believe It or Not?*"

"That's right. A man cracked open an egg and there was a piece of paper in the yolk with a name and phone number printed on it. He called the number and it was a woman in Illinois and they ended up getting married."

"Oddest thing I ever heard."

Dale stirred his coffee, then set his spoon on the napkin. "Asa, I just really believe the Lord is wanting me to move forward on this. I don't know, it's kinda hard to explain, but I feel His hand is on me. Can you help me?"

"What do you need me to do?"

"I need to borrow one of your laying hens," Dale said. "I gotta run some experiments."

Asa said, "Sure, I can give you a laying hen."

"I'll take good care of it."

Asa brought him a chicken the next morning. At first, Dale kept it in his garage, but it kept escaping, so he put it in his cellar.

Dale and his wife could hear the hen at night while they were lying in bed. They could hear it scratching around in the dirt in the crawlspace behind the furnace, looking for worms. So the next morning, Dale went to Grant's Hardware and bought chicken wire and built a pen for the laying hen, next to the furnace.

After a few days, when the chicken was relaxed, he tried to feed it a piece of paper. It wouldn't eat it at first, so Dale tried putting peanut butter on it, but it didn't work. The chicken liked the peanut butter, but it stuck to the roof of its beak. Then Dale tried dabbing maple syrup on the paper, and the chicken ate it right down.

Dale fed the hen one *This is the day the Lord has made, I will rejoice and be glad in it* and one *Jesus wept*.

That very night the chicken laid an egg, which Dale cracked open the next morning for his breakfast. There was a piece of paper in the yolk. As he fished the paper from the egg, Dale's hands trembled. He prayed a quiet prayer, "Thank you, Lord, thank you for this opportunity to serve you."

He unfolded the paper and read, *This is the day Jesus wept.*

Dale tried not to be discouraged. He told his wife, "I think the Lord's testing me to see whether or not I'll stay the course."

He worked out the glitches. Had it all figured out. The shorter the verse the better, and only one verse at a time. He built another pen, added two more chickens, and soon was producing three Scripture eggs a day, which he distributed to the Catholics and the Masons. "Here, have an egg," he told them, handing them an egg.

He wanted nine more laying hens, but Asa Peacock couldn't spare any more, so Dale began looking for venture capitalists — Christian businessmen who not only loved the Lord but also knew a good business deal when they saw one.

"Basically," he told them, "what we have here is a monopoly. We're the only folks in the U.S. of A. making Scripture eggs. The sky's the limit."

But they lacked Dale's vision, and he came up dry.

Then, late one Saturday afternoon, Ellis Hodge came to plow Dale's garden. Every May, Ellis drives his tractor into town to plow the gardens. All winter long people have been thumbing through seed catalogs, yearning for the feel of warm earth. By early April they can't wait. They get out their shovels and try to turn the soil, but after a half hour they are tired and decide to wait for Ellis to come through after he's plowed his fields. He drives up and down the streets of town. If you want your garden plowed, you wave him down and for ten dollars he'll plow your garden. By the time Ellis got to Dale's house in late afternoon, his pockets were jammed with money.

He plowed Dale's garden, then asked Dale about his Scripture egg project.

"I need an investor," Dale told him. "Someone with vision and a heart for the Lord."

Ellis had been looking for a good investment. He'd been reading in the newspaper of the new Internet millionaires. Ellis was not a greedy man, but if he could make a little money and serve the Kingdom, then why not? Plus, he had a daughter to think of now. He needed a legacy, something to leave her.

He asked Dale, "How do you know the eggs have Scripture in them?"

"Some things we just have to take on faith."

"You got that right."

Ellis gave Dale sixty dollars to buy nine laying hens and chicken wire. His investment bought him 49 percent ownership in the Scripture egg business.

Now Dale had twelve chickens going. All of them good layers. Dale told his wife, "It's like they know they're doing the Lord's work."

He stored the eggs in his refrigerator and every Saturday he loaded up five dozen eggs, climbed in his car, sat behind the wheel, and prayed, "Lord, these are your eggs. Just show me where you want them. Lead me, Lord."

Then he would begin driving and passing out eggs, and he wouldn't come home until the eggs were gone.

Dale's dream was to go to Salt Lake City to pass out eggs to the Mormons, or to maybe stand outside a Kingdom Hall up in the city and pass out eggs as the Jehovah's Witnesses left their services.

"Here, have an egg. Take two — they're small."

He wished he had someone to help him. He wished Sam would help him, but Sam didn't seem very interested. Dale wondered about Sam.

He told his wife, "Don't get me wrong — I'm not judging Sam. It's just that he doesn't seem on fire for the Lord. I've asked him several times now to preach on the Scripture egg project, and he won't do it. I know he grew up here and I know folks like him, but I don't see much faith there."

When Ellis Hodge gave him the sixty dollars, Dale took it as a sign that God wanted the Scripture egg project to go forward. He sat in his pew the next Sunday morning and was moved to tears thinking about it — a ministry of his very own after all these years!

He'd begun to worry that the Lord was done with him. But now, in the autumn of his life, God had given him another chance.

Not everyone shared his enthusiasm. One day Sam was complaining to Miriam Hodge about the Scripture egg project. She assured him, "Dale might be a little odd, but even odd people need to feel useful."

"I suppose you're right," Sam said. "I need to be more charitable. I just wish he'd stop pestering the Catholics."

"Yes, I should probably speak to him about that."

Often, Dale would stand during the Quaker silence and talk about how God was using his Scripture eggs. The people would smile and, after worship, shake his hand and encourage him.

Miriam reminded Sam they were Quakers, after all, and we should accept the idea that people might feel led to do something odd. And who's to say, in the economy of God, what is peculiar and what is not? Oddity, like beauty, is in the eye of the beholder. What one person rejects as lunacy, another reveres as truth.

Three

When a Man Loves a Woman

Kyle Weathers returned to Harmony this past spring and is back cutting hair, after being gone a couple years. He'd closed his shop and moved to California to see a woman he'd met on the Internet in a hairstylists' chat room. But it didn't work out and now he's back home and not talking about what happened, despite dogged efforts to uncover the sordid details.

Most of the men were glad to have Kyle back. They were looking chopped up from cutting their own hair. Some of the more progressive men had gone to Kathy at the Kut 'N' Kurl. At the time, it seemed a drastic step, to have your hair cut in a beauty shop. The men were a little uneasy at first, but Kathy is easy on the eyes and she runs her hands through your hair to plump it up. You're sorry when the haircut is finished. Kyle never runs his hands through your hair, and you wouldn't want him to. You'd look at him kind of funny if he did.

Another difference is that Kathy asks how you want your hair cut. Kyle has one haircut he gives to all the men — a buzz cut with whitewalls. One-Style Kyle, they call him.

Kathy asks how you want your hair cut, and if you aren't sure, she offers suggestions of haircuts she's seen in the movies.

"Honey, you remind me of Harrison Ford in a rugged and handsome kind of way. Let's try his *Raiders of the Lost Ark* look."

Or she might say, "Did anyone ever tell you that you look just like that new James Bond guy? With the right haircut, you could be his twin."

Kyle would never do that, and the only person you look like when Kyle is done cutting your hair is Sergeant Carter from *Gomer Pyle*. But Kyle does have his merits, one of them being his ability to keep a secret, which is why Wayne Fleming told him about being in love with Deena Morrison.

Deena had moved to town the year before, fresh from law school. Twenty-five years old and the picture of beauty. She'd opened a law practice, but people were suspicious of a beautiful woman lawyer and her practice folded after a few months. That's when she opened the Legal Grounds Coffee Shop. She sold coffee and answered any two legal questions for ten dollars.

Wayne loves her but he wants it kept

quiet, on account of he's still married, though he hasn't seen his wife for over a year. She ran off with a trucker, and he hasn't heard from her. At least that's the rumor going around town. It's just him and the kids in their trailer east of town. Wayne feels guilty even thinking about Deena, being a married man and all, but it can't be helped. She's so nice, and he's so lonely.

So when he was in Kyle's shop getting his hair cut and it was just the two of them in there and the subject turned to women, Wayne let it slip.

It was the music that loosened his tongue. Ever since Kyle returned from California, he's been listening to old love songs on his record player in the barbershop. He plays "I Left My Heart in San Francisco." The 1962 Tony Bennett version. If Kyle is there by himself, he sings along in a wistful voice.

Kyle told Wayne a little about the woman in California. As he confided his love, he began to weep. When he was in California, he joined a men's group where he met his inner child and learned to cry.

Then Percy Sledge sang "When a Man Loves a Woman" and that's when Wayne, his defenses down, told Kyle about Deena and his feelings for her. "It's wishful thinking," Wayne admitted. "What would a beautiful woman like that see in me? She probably doesn't even know I'm alive."

"You're probably right," Kyle agreed. "We're nothing but playthings to them. Toys for the heart, that's all."

"I'm a fool for even thinking about a woman, after what my wife did," Wayne said.

But he lies in bed and dreams about marching over to the Legal Grounds Coffee Shop, throwing open the door, striding across the wooden floor, drawing Deena to him, and kissing her flush on her lips. Just like in the movies. Just like Rhett Butler and Scarlett O'Hara in *Gone with the Wind*.

Then his alarm clock sounds and he gets up, cleans the trailer, and fixes supper for the kids. Then he goes to the Kroger, where he works nights, mopping the floors.

Wayne has three children — a boy and two girls. Right in a row. Adam is seven, Rachel six, and Kate five. A neighbor lady watches them when Wayne is at work and once a month when Kyle cuts his hair.

Things are leveling out. When their mommy ran off, the kids kept asking when she'd be home. They'd cry at bedtime. Now they're kind of forgetting about her. After a while, Wayne took the old family picture

38

down from the wall, drove the kids into the city to Sears, and had a new photo taken of just him and the kids.

Sometimes, after the children are in bed and he has the night off, he goes outside and sits on the trailer steps. He leaves the door open so he can hear the kids. Sitting there, listening to the crickets, he contemplates life with Deena. He laughs at the craziness of it. She is a lawyer and owns her own business. I mop floors at the Kroger and live in a trailer with three kids. What do I have to offer that fine woman? Not a thing. Besides, I'm a married man. I need to put her out of my mind.

But he can't.

There's a college in the next county. Once, on his day off, Wayne drove over and met with a woman in the admissions department. He handed her his high-school records. She gazed at them, then smiled at Wayne and said, "You know, Mr. Fleming, college isn't for everyone."

"I'm a hard worker," Wayne told her. "I have a family now, and I need to make something of myself. I can do the work."

Wayne had always wanted to be a teacher. He had wanted to go to college, but in the summer after high school he'd gotten his girlfriend pregnant. They were married, and Wayne went to work instead. That was seven years ago.

His parents won't let him forget. They talk about Wayne's brother, who went to college, and how well he's doing. "That could have been you," they tell Wayne.

The college let him in on probation. He takes a class at a time, one day a week, and will graduate in twelve years. Then he'll become a teacher and an example to his children.

He wants better for them. He reads to them and goes without so his kids can wear new clothes and look nice. He takes them to the museums in the city and teaches his son to open the door for his sisters.

He told them, "We may be poor, but we're not ill-mannered."

The week after his haircut at Kyle's, Wayne dressed Adam, Rachel, and Kate in their nicest clothes and drove to the Legal Grounds Coffee Shop. It was a Saturday morning. Deena cleaned off a table for them and — to Wayne's deep joy — sat down at their table, admiring the children. Wayne was faint with bliss.

Then Kate, the five-year-old, took Deena's hand and said, "Our mommy left us. Can you be our mommy?"

There was an awkward quiet. Deena said,

"It's not quite that easy, honey. It doesn't work like that." Her face turned red.

Wayne was embarrassed, having his children troll for a mother in public. He gathered them up, said good-bye to Deena, and drove home.

He walked past the Legal Grounds often after that, looking in the window and watching her pour coffee. But he'd stay outside. Deena would smile at him. He'd smile back, then walk away.

Why torture myself? he'd think.

He was glad Kyle was back from California. It gave him someone to talk with.

A few weeks later Wayne sat in the barber's chair while Kyle buzzed his hair and talked about his Internet girlfriend from California.

It was his fault, Kyle admitted. He never should have gone out there. "I'm thinking now if we'd just have stuck to the Internet and not tried to meet one another face to face, we'd still be together."

"What kind of life would that have been?" Wayne asked. "Wasn't getting to know her worth the risk?"

Kyle didn't think so. "I was happier just dreaming about her. Then I had to go and act on it, and now my heart's broken.

41

Maybe you're better off not asking Deena out. At least this way you still have your dream. I don't even have that anymore."

Wayne looked at Kyle. Fifty-five years old and all alone, with not a prospect in sight. That would be him one day, if he didn't act. Now.

He rose from the chair and said, "I'm going to risk it. I'm going to ask Deena Morrison for a date. Right now." He strode from the barbershop.

"She'll crush your soul," Kyle yelled after him.

Wayne marched down past the Rexall and the Baptist church, crossed Main Street against the light, and flung open the door of the Legal Grounds Coffee Shop. It was empty except for Deena, who was sweeping the wooden floor.

She stared at Wayne. Wayne stared back. He didn't know what to say so he just stood there, looking.

"Why are you wearing a barber's cape?" she asked.

Dumb, dumb, dumb, Wayne thought. Wayne Fleming, you are a moron.

"Uh, I was getting a haircut."

"It looks nice so far."

"Thank you. Kyle's not quite done with it yet. Uh, I have a question to ask you."

"Yes?" Deena smiled at him.

Oh, she had a beautiful smile. Wayne's insides shuddered. He felt his bowels release momentarily.

"Could I please have a cup of coffee?" he asked.

She poured him a cup.

Wayne sat a table. Deena went back to sweeping. He gazed at her over the top of his coffee mug, hoping she'd sweep her way toward him. She moved closer. This is it, he thought. "Uh, say, Deena, how would you like to go somewhere with me?"

"Where would you like to go?"

He hadn't thought that far ahead. It would have to be somewhere cheap. He didn't have any money.

"I was thinking maybe we could go to church," Wayne said.

"Church? Did you say church?"

"Sure. Why not?"

Dumb, dumb, dumb, Wayne thought. You just asked Deena Morrison on a date to church. Dumb, dumb, dumb.

"Where do you go to church?" Deena asked.

Dumb, dumb, dumb. I don't even have a church. "Uh . . . well . . . I went to the Quaker church this past Easter. Maybe we could go there."

"I'd like that." Deena smiled at Wayne. He smiled at her and his insides shuddered.

He walked back to Kyle's to finish his haircut.

"She said yes," he told Kyle.

Kyle shook his head, sadly. "Your life is ruined. You watch and see. You should have just stuck with your dreams," he said, then picked up his clippers. "But if you insist on ruining your life, let's at least make sure you have a good haircut while you do it."

Wayne lay awake that night. Here he was, a married man, taking another woman to the Lord's house. God's gonna strike me dead, he thought.

The next morning was Sunday. Wayne rose early, showered, and shaved. He woke up his children. They ate breakfast. Then he gave them a bath, combed their hair, and dressed them in their nicest clothes. He dabbed on some Old Spice and put on his one suit. They drove into town to Deena's house.

She answered the door. She was radiant.

"Do you mind if we walk?" Wayne asked.

They walked down the sidewalk, underneath the trees. It was a pleasant spring morning, not too hot. The dogwoods were in bloom.

"It's a beautiful day," Deena said.

He gazed at her. "Absolutely stunning."

Rachel and Kate held Deena's hand. Wayne rested his hand on Adam's cowlicky head and stole glances at Deena.

They sat in the seventh row, just behind the Fern Hampton pew. Deena on one end and Wayne on the other with the children in between. Wayne's right arm rested on the back of the pew, Deena's left arm across the back of the pew. Their hands accidentally brushed. Wayne's face turned red. Deena smiled and kept her hand on top of Wayne's for a brief moment. Well, if God's gonna strike me, this would be the time, he thought. But nothing happened. All he felt was joy, and a little confusion.

He sat in the pew thinking how messy love was. He'd loved his wife. Then she'd left him and the desolation nearly killed him. For a while he was angry, but that passed. Now he pitied her. A small part of him still loved her. He'd be sitting in the chair at Kyle's, listening to the songs, and would miss her and want her back. He'd remember sliding the ring on her finger. Till death do us part. Whoever wrote that had the order wrong. It isn't death that causes the parting. It's the parting that causes death. Wayne had felt dead for so long.

But sitting there in church, with Deena's hand touching his, Wayne didn't feel dead anymore. He felt wonderfully alive. During the Quaker silence, he dreamed of marrying Deena and graduating from college and teaching. Imagined he and Deena tucking the kids into bed and kissing their scrubbed heads and telling them stories. Then he thought of lying in bed with Deena and talking and maybe doing the things husbands and wives do.

His insides shuddered at the thought of it.

He grew afraid God would strike him dead for thinking such things in church. He tried to think about something else, but couldn't. All he could think about was Deena.

Dear sweet Lord, he prayed silently, give me this woman and let me know some joy. Please, Lord. I'm so lonely.

Then he turned his wrist, and Deena's hand settled into his. He glanced at her. Oh, she was lovely. She was watching him, smiling a shy smile.

It must be the haircut, he thought.

Then he didn't think anything. He just sat there, in the seventh pew, his hand in hers, nauseous with love.

Four

Sam's Fading Faith

Something had been wrong since Easter, almost two months ago. A cloudy desolation had swept over Sam Gardner, fast as a summer storm, raging in and pounding down.

He'd read an article in a Christian magazine about the ten warning signs of depression. He had seven of them. A note at the bottom of the article read:

If you exhibit seven of these symptoms, you are at risk for depression. Please see your pastor for guidance.

But Sam *was* the pastor. It's hopeless, he thought. Hopeless. That was another sign of depression — feelings of hopelessness. Now he had eight signs of depression.

Sam had thought about getting counseling. The mental-health agency rented a room in the upstairs of the *Harmony Herald* building. Bob Miles, the editor of the *Herald*, liked to sit at his desk and look out the window at the town square and write about what he saw in his column, "The Bobservation Post." If you visited the mental-health center, chances were good you'd be written about.

Sam could just imagine what Bob would write:

People are up and about early this morning. I see Jessie Peacock walking into the Kroger as Fern Hampton is walking out. Jessie and Fern stop to visit in front of the bags of peat moss stacked on the sidewalk. There's Vinny Toricelli, washing windows at the Coffee Cup. Kyle Weathers is sitting out front of his barbershop, reading a magazine. I see Sam Gardner coming down the sidewalk. He's stopping here at the *Herald* for a visit. No, he's heading upstairs to the mental-health center.

That's why Sam couldn't go to the mental-health center.

He was going to talk with Barbara, but didn't want to worry her, so he talked with his father instead, on a Saturday morning in early June. He hadn't planned to, but he'd been walking past his parents' house on his way to the meetinghouse and saw his father in the garage, repairing their wooden screen door.

Sam walked up the driveway and into the garage. "Hey, Dad, what you doing?"

48

"What's it look like?"

"Dad, I was hoping maybe we could talk."

His father kept working. "Whatcha need, Sam?"

"Could you put down the hammer, please?"

Charlie set down the hammer and turned toward Sam, concerned. "What is it, son? Is anything wrong?"

"I'm not quite sure. It's just that lately I haven't been feeling well."

"Have you been to see Doc Neely?"

"No, it's not that kind of not feeling well. I'm feeling depressed."

His father laughed. "Depressed? Is that all? For crying out loud, what have you got to be depressed about? You got it easy. Why, when I was your age, I didn't have time to be depressed. I had too much work to do. Maybe that's your problem. Maybe you don't have enough to do."

That wasn't Sam's problem. He had more than enough to do. It never let up. Sixty hours a week. His phone ringing off the hook. Plus, in the two months since Goal-Setting Sunday, Dale Hinshaw had been hounding him about the Scripture egg project.

"Sam," Dale had said one Sunday after

49

worship, "I think we oughta get together on Monday mornings to discuss what you need to do for the Scripture egg project."

"Mondays aren't good days. It's my one day off. I like spending the day with my family."

"Bring them along. Who knows, maybe they can help too."

The next morning, at eight o'clock, Dale had knocked on their door.

"Hi, Dale, what brings you by here on my day off?" Sam asked.

"I stopped by the meetinghouse, but you weren't there. If you want to meet here, that's fine with me." Dale walked into the house. "Say, is that bacon I smell? Why don't we eat a little breakfast first. It's hard to think lofty thoughts on an empty stomach."

Every Monday since, Dale had stopped by to discuss his Scripture egg project. He'd stay all morning, until Sam could edge him out the door. And every Monday Dale would ask Sam to preach about the Scripture egg project.

"I will if the Lord leads me," Sam promised.

But lately the Lord hadn't led Sam on much of anything. He usually wrote his sermons on Fridays. He would think about his sermon all week long, then on Fridays he'd arrive at the meetinghouse by eight in the morning. Frank, his secretary, was always waiting with coffee. They'd drink their coffee, sitting in Sam's office. At eight-thirty Sam would say, "Well, it's sermon day. I'd better get at it."

But ever since Easter, Sam had been struggling with what to say. He was tired of writing sermons. One Friday in early June, he figured he had written over seven hundred sermons in his fourteen years of ministry.

What can I say that hasn't already been said? he thought. I'm tired of words. Talk, talk, talk. That's all we do in the church. I've already preached more sermons than Jesus did.

That was the week he decided he wasn't going to preach.

Sam stood at the pulpit that Sunday and spoke to the congregation.

"Quakers believe God leads us to speak, and that unless God leads us to speak, we shouldn't speak. God did not give me a message this week, so I will not speak. If God has led any of you to speak, we would welcome your message."

Then he sat down.

People looked at one another, puzzled. Although it was true no one should preach without being led, it was also true that God had been in the habit of speaking to Sam every Friday in his office between the hours of eight-thirty and noon.

The congregation sat in a fidgety silence. Always before, the Quaker silence had been tolerated because they knew it wouldn't last, that Sam would eventually rise to his feet and bring a message. But this was silence with no end in sight. This was uncomfortable, bordering on painful. What would happen? How long would they have to sit there?

All across the meeting room, people asked themselves, Lord, are you leading me to speak today?

They listened for God's voice and were relieved not to hear it.

Then they began to pray for God to lead someone — anyone — to speak.

Dale Hinshaw cleared his throat and stood up from his pew.

Several dozen people told the Lord that Dale wasn't who they'd had in mind.

It was Mr. and Mrs. Dale Hinshaw's fortieth wedding anniversary. He told how they'd met as students at the Ozark School of the Scriptures. How they'd married right after college and gone to pastor a church, but that it didn't work out. His throat caught as he spoke. He hadn't intended to reveal this much, but standing there, speaking, he could scarcely contain himself.

The congregation was amazed. Dale Hinshaw, a minister? They tried to imagine that.

Dale told how guilty he'd felt for leaving the ministry but that now, with his Scripture eggs, he believed God was giving him a second chance.

"I won't be here next Sunday. I'll be at the Unitarians up in the city passing out my Scripture eggs. I sure could use some help. If the Lord's nudging you that way, come see me after church."

Then he sat down, just as Fern Hampton stood up. Fern had never spoken during worship. They leaned forward, eager to hear her message from the Lord. She placed her hands on the back of the pew in front of her, steadying herself.

She paused. Every eye was on her. Her voice rose up from the sixth row.

"I've been thinking of the new bathroom vanity we'll be buying for the ladies' rest room. As long as we're all here together, I'd like to take a quick vote. Men, this is for the ladies only. Ladies, if you'd like a white vanity, raise your hand."

Bea Majors queried from her seat behind the organ, "Is it white-white or cream-white?"

"White-white."

Twenty-one ladies raised their hands. Fern counted once, then counted again just to be sure.

"Okay, that's twenty-one votes for a white vanity. Now the other option is an oak-grain vanity. Ladies, raise your hands if you want an oak-grain vanity."

Fern scanned the meeting room, counting twenty-nine upraised hands.

"Oak-grained it is," she announced, then sat back down, her sacred duty accomplished.

Sam sat in his chair behind the pulpit, his head in his hands. No wonder I'm discouraged, he thought. He stood up before anyone else could speak. "Let us pray." They bowed their heads while Sam prayed for God to bless their meeting. And soon, he prayed silently.

"Amen," he concluded.

"Amen," mumbled the congregation.

Sam didn't stay to talk. He slipped out the back door and walked home by himself, taking the long way home. He wasn't ready to face his wife. Didn't want to talk about what had happened. Mostly, he wanted to think.

When Sam had been in seminary, he'd dreamed of pastoring struggling churches and transforming them by the power of his words. Back then, Sam had loved words. He believed if he said the right words, his church would grow and lives would be changed.

But when Sam said the right words, people grew mad, and after a while it became easier to say the agreeable words. He discovered people weren't interested in change, but in stability.

For seven hundred sermons he chased after the perfect, elusive words that would open hearts. But the words never came.

Now Sam was tired of words.

He went home and sat on the porch. Barbara came out of the house. She sat down next to Sam on the porch swing. "What's wrong, honey?" she asked.

"I can't keep this up."

"Can't keep what up?"

"Being a pastor. I can't keep it up. I'm absolutely empty."

"Then quit."

"I can't quit. What will I do? Being a pastor is all I know to do."

"Find something else to do."

"Look, I'm thirty-nine years old. I've got

a family to take care of and a mortgage to pay. It's a little too late to find something else to do."

They didn't talk for the longest time. They just pushed back and forth in the swing. Somewhere down the block, a screen door banged.

"Maybe I should find another church," Sam said.

"That would work for about a year. Then you'd be empty again. Why are you empty?"

Sam knew why, but he was afraid to say it out loud. He'd known since Easter why he was empty. He remembered the very moment. It had happened in Easter worship. He had been preaching about the power of God to overcome death, but as he preached he realized he no longer believed it. He'd wanted to sit down right then, but feared what people might think.

Instead, he finished his sermon and sat in his chair behind the pulpit, asking himself, If God can overcome death, why are so many of His churches dead?

It was a question he couldn't answer.

And that's when Sam Gardner had stopped believing.

In everything he'd once believed.

Five

Hard Times

When the elders of Harmony Friends Meeting put lottery tickets in the church bulletins to increase attendance, they never imagined Jessie Peacock would win five million dollars.

Most people would have been thrilled, but Jessie was miserable. She didn't believe in the lottery. She thought it was a tax on idiocy, so when she won that money she believed God was giving her a platform. She went to the statehouse so the governor could present her the check, but when the TV man told her to smile and shake the governor's hand, she tore the check in half and scolded the governor for duping the ignorant poor.

The state mailed her letters asking her to take the money. She tore the letters up and mailed them back. That was last year. Jessie had hoped God might reward her faithfulness and make life a little easier for her and her husband, Asa, but that had not happened.

Asa and Jessie Peacock farm south of town. Last summer the hog cholera came through and killed all their pigs. Then it didn't rain for two months, and their crops dried up. This past winter Asa took a job in the county seat, working nights on the kill line at the poultry plant. Worried, frantic chickens would hurl toward Asa on the conveyor belt. He would grab every fourth one and lop its head off. "Nothing personal," he told them. "Just doing my job."

But Asa was troubled. When he was a little boy he had a pet chicken, Mr. Peeps, who had followed him everywhere and slept in his bed. Asa was grateful Mr. Peeps wasn't alive to see how far he had fallen.

Asa wasn't averse to killing the occasional chicken for his own consumption. It was the wholesale slaughter that troubled him. The ruthless organization of it. He worried the chickens wouldn't forgive him.

He began to have chicken nightmares. One night he dreamed he was riding on a conveyor belt, and a giant chicken grabbed him by the feet and lopped his head off.

He told Dale Hinshaw about his nightmares one morning at the Coffee Cup.

"Sounds like post-dramatic stress syndrome to me," Dale said. "You see it mostly in war veterans and schoolteachers, but occasionally with poultry workers."

The next Sunday during church Asa

prayed for God to stop the dreams. But that night he dreamed he was back on the kill line and, just before he killed a chicken, the chicken looked deep into Asa's eyes. He saw the chicken's lips move and heard the chicken cry out, "It's me, Asa. Mr. Peeps. Don't you remember me?"

In the dream, the other chickens crowded around Asa's feet, pecking his ankles.

Asa woke up sweating and lay awake for quite some time. He heard the downstairs clock chime two o'clock, then three. Then he fell asleep.

In the morning his ankles were sore. He pulled off his socks. His ankles were covered with little red marks. He went downstairs to the kitchen, showed Jessie his ankles, and told her about his dream. He asked her what she thought.

"I think you should quit."

But he couldn't. They needed the money. Instead, Asa gave up sleep. At night he worked at the poultry plant; then he'd come home and work the farm.

By June they were down to three hundred dollars in their savings account. Then Jessie got another letter from the lottery people asking if she'd changed her mind. This time, she didn't tear it up. Instead, she stuck

59

it on the front of the refrigerator. The letter said they had until the end of August to claim the money. She'd open the refrigerator to get out the milk, and her eyes would fall on that letter. Five million dollars. She'd think about Asa working two jobs and not sleeping.

She pondered if winning the lottery was God's way of helping them and that maybe she'd been too hasty in refusing the check. She wished she hadn't torn the check in half on television. She would have to eat a lot of crow if she cashed the lottery check now.

She wondered if this was God's way of humbling her.

Then, one July morning during the haying season, their tractor broke down. Asa had to borrow a team of mules and a wagon from their Amish neighbor to finish bringing the hay bales to the barn. There was a creek that ran between the house and the barn. Asa would guide the mules over the bridge toward the barn and up the earthen ramp into the barn.

His great-grandfather had built the barn. It had his name over the doorway — *Abraham Peacock* — and the year the barn was built — *1898*. Over the fireplace in their house was a picture of Abraham Peacock standing in front of his new barn, looking

60

prosperous.

Over a hundred years later, the barn was still standing. Asa loved that barn. Loved the animal smell and the swirls of hay on the floor. When he was a boy, he and his brothers would make forts in the loft using hay bales. They'd tie off ropes from the beams and swing down from the loft. The old ropes still hung from the beams, rope icicles reaching to the ground.

Asa was urging the mules across the bridge toward the barn when the mules quit. He looped a rope around their necks and pulled, but they dug in. Jessie came out of the house and pushed the mules from behind, but they stood fast.

Asa said, "Well, if they're going to take a break, we will too." They went inside to eat lunch.

They ate lunch looking out the window at the mules.

"Stubborn creatures," Asa muttered.

After lunch, he phoned Ellis Hodge, seeking counsel. Ellis Hodge was a fount of information.

Ellis said, "Seems to me I read something in last year's almanac about how to move a stubborn mule."

Asa loved the almanac. He had built a shelf in the living room to hold all his almanacs. While Jessie washed the lunch dishes, Asa pulled last year's almanac from the shelf and began to thumb through it.

"I'll be," he yelled to Jessie. "Did you know that if the north side of a beech tree is sweaty, it's gonna rain?"

Jessie hadn't known that.

Asa read on.

"Say, here's a good idea. It says to save your old rubber gloves and cut them up for rubber bands. Do you do that?"

Jessie yelled back, "I don't use rubber gloves."

Asa turned the page. "Hey, this is interesting. What do you do with the empty toilet paper rolls?"

"I throw them away."

"It says here you should use them as sachets in drawers and closets."

"I'll try to remember that."

"Did you know that if a chicken stands on one leg, the weather will turn cold?"

"I had no idea."

"Yep, and if there are lots of dogwood blossoms, it'll be a good corn crop."

"Imagine that."

"Here it is!" Asa shouted. "To move a stubborn mule, light a small fire underneath the mule and it will move."

He walked into the kitchen and asked

Jessie where they kept the matches. She opened the cabinet over their stove and handed Asa an Ohio Blue Tip.

They went outside. Jessie watched as Asa took an armload of hay from the wagon and piled it underneath the mules. He took the match from his pocket and scratched it on his zipper. He touched the match to the hay.

The mules stood fast while the first wisps of smoke began to curl around their bellies. As the fire grew, they began to rock back and forth.

"There they go!" Asa yelled.

The mules lunged toward the barn, but not far enough or fast enough. They stopped just as the wagon was over the fire. The dry floorboards of the wagon began to kindle.

Asa dashed to the barn for a bucket. He hurried to the creek to fill the bucket. The mules looked back, alarmed. They saw the flames and felt the heat, and their strength was renewed. They bolted for the barn, pulling the burning wagon behind them. The flames climbed up the ropes into the loft. Before long, the loft was ablaze.

Jessie and Asa unharnessed the mules from the wagon and drove them from the barn. Then Jessie ran inside to phone the fire department. A while later they could hear the fire whistle from town sound over the fields. By the time the volunteer fire department arrived, the whole barn was aflame.

When the pumper went dry, the firemen pumped water from the creek. It took them two hours to put out the fire. The only part of the barn left standing was the doorway. You could just make out the numbers — *1898*. Asa and Jessie stood before the smoldering ruins, holding each other. That was the picture Bob Miles snapped to run in the *Harmony Herald*.

"How did she burn?" Bob inquired, his pen poised, ready to write.

Asa had seen what happened to people who did dumb things in Harmony. In 1913, his great-grandfather, Abraham Peacock, had driven a Model T through the Grant Hardware Emporium plate glass window while pulling back on the steering wheel and yelling "Whoa!" at the top of his lungs. He lived thirty more years and never lived it down.

"I'd rather not say," he answered Bob.

Bob wrote on his pad of paper, *The fire was of a suspicious origin.*

The next day was Sunday. Jessie and Asa

went to town to church. Everyone there had heard about their barn.

Dale Hinshaw, their insurance agent, reminded them to come by his office to put in a claim.

"Just exactly how did the fire start?" he asked Asa. "I need to know for when I fill out the forms."

"I'd rather not say. Do the insurance people have to know?"

"Only if you want your money."

"Can't we just leave that part of the form blank?"

"Not if you want to be paid."

"In that case, I don't think we'll be filing a claim."

That night as Asa and Jessie lay in bed, Jessie began to weep. "First the pigs, then the crops. Now we've lost our barn."

Asa held Jessie to him, stroking her head.

"What a mess we're in," she sniffed. "If I hadn't gone on television and ripped up that check and talked against the lottery, I could cash that check and we'd be fine."

"There, there, it's not your fault. If I'd have told Dale how the barn burned, we'd at least have the insurance money."

"Foolish pride. That's our biggest problem. Foolish pride." Then she sat straight up in bed. "I don't care what people think, I'm going to take that lottery money. I'm tired of you having those horrible dreams and working two jobs."

"Stop that talk. You were right not to take the money. We'll be fine. The dogwood blossoms were heavy this spring. According to the almanac that means a good corn crop."

"You'll have to forgive me for not putting much faith in the almanac."

They fell asleep. Jessie dreamed about cashing in her ticket and building Asa a new barn, having his picture taken in front of it, and hanging the picture over their fireplace. Asa dreamed about the mules lighting a fire underneath him while the chickens looked on, clucking their approval.

The next morning they sat at the table, eating their breakfast and gazing out the window. Every now and then, a small plume of smoke would rise up from the burned timbers of the barn.

Asa sighed.

Jessie said, "Well, at least there's lots of dogwood blossoms."

"Does that mean you won't be cashing the check?"

"Oh, I probably won't."

They sat quiet. Jessie drinking her coffee, Asa reading the almanac.

Asa spoke out of the stillness, "You know, honey, it's easy to have convictions when times are good. But what really counts is if you can keep your convictions when times are hard."

"I suppose you're right."

They finished their breakfast, washed the dishes, then walked through their fields. The corn was up past their knees.

Asa said, "According to the almanac, corn should be knee-high by the Fourth of July."

"Seems I've heard that."

They're praying for a good crop. But that letter is still hanging on their refrigerator, just in case.

Six

The Legacy

It was early July, one month since Sam Gardner had told his father he was depressed. The day Sam dropped by, Charlie Gardner had been in his garage, fixing his wooden screen door. He'd laid the door flat across two sawhorses and was replacing the screen, remembering back to when Sam was a little boy and had pushed the screen out.

He recalled getting mad and yelling at Sam to be careful, and Sam crying. Then he'd felt like a jerk, so he walked little Sam the four blocks to Grant's Hardware, where they bought more screen and wood trim. Then he took Sam to the Dairy Queen and bought him an ice cream cone with sprinkles. Then he let Sam help him paint the door and taught him how to open it so the screen didn't get pushed out.

Thirty years and two screen doors ago.

He'd been halfway through the latest job when Sam came by and confided about being depressed. Charlie had spent the next two days laboring over the door and worrying about Sam, mad at himself for not being more sympathetic.

When Sam had told him about being depressed, he'd laughed. Laughed at his own son. He hated himself as soon as he did it. He hadn't meant to laugh, but Sam's candor had startled him and he'd laughed. Sam had been hurt, he could tell. He'd hurt his son.

He'd felt terrible ever since.

Charlie was proud of his boy. He sat in church on Sunday mornings and listened to Sam preach and marveled, That's my boy. Where did he learn this? How did he get so smart?

But he'd never told Sam he was proud of him. He wanted to, but he couldn't find the words. On Christmas Eve the year before, he had hugged Sam. He'd almost told him then how proud he was of him, what with his mouth being close to Sam's ear, but he didn't. He just squeezed Sam a little harder.

He knows I'm proud of him, Charlie assured himself.

But for the past month, he had been watching Sam closely, looking for signs of depression. He'd gone to the library to read about depression. Miss Rudy, the librarian, had hovered about him, asking if he needed help looking something up.

He didn't want to tell Miss Rudy he

wanted to read about depression. She'd think he was depressed and would march him down to the mental-health office over the *Herald*. She was pushy that way.

Charlie had found an article about the warning signs of depression — loss of appetite, loss of interest in work, unusual irritability, diminished ability to concentrate, and difficulty sleeping.

The next Sunday Sam had stood in meeting and told the congregation he wasn't going to preach. The warning sign *Loss of interest in work* leapt to his father's mind.

He'd peered at Sam more closely. There were dark circles under Sam's eyes.

Difficulty sleeping!

Charlie phoned Sam the next morning to meet him for lunch at the Legal Grounds Coffee Shop, even though Charlie didn't like the Legal Grounds. They didn't serve hamburgers or onion rings like the Coffee Cup. Instead, Deena served croissant sandwiches and spinach salads and vegetarian pizzas. But Sam liked it, and that's what mattered.

They'd met for lunch. Sam had been distracted. He'd pushed his salad around his plate. Even Deena Morrison had noticed.

"Not hungry today, Sam?" she asked.

"I've been a little off my feed," he said. *Loss of appetite!*

Charlie had encouraged Sam to take up a hobby — stamp collecting or gardening or maybe flying model airplanes.

Charlie's hobby was his red Farmall tractor. Years before, he'd driven past Ellis Hodge's farm and seen the tractor sitting by the road with a *For Sale* sign leaning against the front tire. He'd stopped his car to look at it. It was a 1939 Farmall Model M, just like the tractor Charlie's father had used on their farm. He climbed up in the seat, closed his eyes, and was transported to his youth.

Ellis was asking two hundred dollars. Charlie went to the bank, got the money and paid Ellis, and drove the tractor home, with Ellis following behind in his car. Charlie didn't tell his wife — he just did it. The tractor was in pretty rough shape, but he'd fixed it up. Took him two years. Then he fired up his rototiller and made a flower bed in his front yard; he parked the tractor in the middle of it and planted marigolds all around it. A monument to the Farmall.

He likes to sit on his porch after supper and gaze at his monument. Three or four times a year, someone will knock on his door and offer to buy it.

"It's not for sale," he tells them.

His wife wants him to sell it, but he won't hear of it. It would be like selling a child. Charlie loves his tractor. He drives it in the Fourth of July parade and in the Corn and Sausage Days parade the second week of September.

The Fourth of July parade is the highlight of his year. The day before, he waxes the tractor and tunes the engine. He mounts flags on the fenders. He has his wife, Gloria, take a picture of him standing in front of his tractor. He pastes the picture in a scrapbook. Twenty-eight pictures in all, one for each year he's owned the Farmall.

In 1976, Charlie painted the tractor red, white, and blue for the Bicentennial. The newspaper from the city took his picture as he swung in place behind Harvey Muldock's 1951 Plymouth Cranbrook convertible. Even though the picture was in black and white, it still radiated glory. He'd clipped the picture from the paper and mounted it in his scrapbook. During the winter, he takes the scrapbook down from the closet shelf and thumbs through it, reminiscing.

He stores the tractor in Ellis's barn through the winter. He visits it on Saturday mornings, then drives it home the first week of April. That's the sign that spring has come, when Charlie Gardner drives his 1939 Farmall Model M tractor in from the Hodges' farm west of town.

Charlie had been hard at work getting ready for this year's Fourth of July parade. He sanded the tractor down, borrowed Harvey Muldock's air compressor, and sprayed a new coat of Farmall Red on it. It's never looked better. Early of a morning, Charlie sits on his porch drinking coffee and watching his tractor.

This is what Sam needs, he says to himself. He needs some beauty in his life he can lose himself in.

On the morning of the Fourth, Charlie mounted the flags on the fenders and wiped the engine clean. At nine-thirty, he drove the tractor to the elementary school, where the parade was to begin. He took his place behind Harvey's Cranbrook, just in front of the school band. It's hard to hear the band over the tractor, which no one seems to mind.

The parade went north on Washington Street, past Owen Stout's law office and the Legal Grounds, then turned west at the *Harmony Herald* office, and ran down Main Street past the Rexall and Kivett's Five and

Dime. He waved and threw Tootsie Rolls to the children.

It's the same parade every year. Harvey Muldock in his convertible, Charlie Gardner on his tractor, the high-school band, the Odd Fellows Lodge, and the Shriners on their motorbikes. The veterans bring up the rear, their backs straight, their heads high.

There is much cheering. People appreciate the effort. The Shriners have brushed the lint from their fezzes and combed the tassels. Charlie has waxed his tractor. The veterans have pressed their pants and shaved their necks. The streets have been swept. Flags flutter from the lightposts. A deep pride hangs in the air. And Charlie and his tractor are in the thick of it. What a glory!

The parade is his legacy. Three years before, a certain town board member had visited New York City to view the Macy's Thanksgiving Day parade. At the next town board meeting he'd suggested leaving the tractor out of the parade.

"You don't see a tractor in the Macy's parade," he said. "It makes us look like hicks. They don't do that in New York City."

"This isn't New York City," someone pointed out.

The next election, Charlie ran against him on the anti–New York City platform and won handsomely. He's now the town board president.

But Charlie's growing older and keeping up the tractor is hard work. It's not easy being a legacy. People don't say it, but they expect the tractor to be more resplendent each year — the paint to gleam a little brighter, the engine to purr a little smoother. The pressure's getting to Charlie. He wonders what will happen to his tractor when he's gone. He's thought of having it buried with him, maybe have Johnny Mackey at the funeral home prop him up in the seat for an eternal tractor ride.

The morning after the Fourth of July parade, Charlie's tractor was back in place, gleaming amongst the marigolds. Sam stopped to visit. He brought his two boys, Levi and Addison. They climbed on the tractor while Sam and his father sat on the porch. Watching them, Charlie laughed. "You were about Levi's age when I bought that tractor."

Sam smiled. "I remember when you brought it home. Mom didn't talk for two whole days."

75

"Yeah, well, she's over it now."

They fell quiet, watching the boys. Then Charlie said, "Son, last month you told me you were . . . uh . . . not feeling well. Are things any better?"

"Not much. Barbara says I'm having a midlife crisis. She thinks you were right about me needing a hobby. Maybe I ought to buy an old sports car and fix it up."

His father thought for a moment, then said, "I was about your age when I bought my tractor." He studied his tractor. "Isn't she a beaut?"

Sam didn't think so. When he was a teenager, it had embarrassed him to have a tractor in his front yard. He'd bring home girls to meet his parents, and there would be the red Farmall. But he'd never said anything to his father. He hadn't wanted to hurt his feelings.

"Yeah, she's a beaut all right," Sam said.

Sam and his boys visited for a while longer, then walked home.

That afternoon, Charlie drove the tractor to Sam's house and arranged it in Sam's front yard beneath the oak trees next to the flagstone walk. Sam and Barbara and the boys came out of the house. The boys yelled and ran to climb on the tractor.

"What's with the tractor, Dad?" Sam

asked.

His father paused, then cleared his throat. "Well, son, I've decided I want you to have it."

The idea had come to him during the Fourth of July parade, while the people waved at him and called his name. The delight of it, to be acknowledged and loved by your fellow citizens.

This is what Sam needs, he'd said to himself. Affirmation. Acceptance.

That's when the thought had hit. Give Sam the tractor! Give your son a hobby. But more than a hobby, a legacy!

Charlie stood beside the tractor, his hand resting on the fender. "It's yours, son. I hope it brings you the happiness it's brought me."

He got choked up as he said it. Parting with his tractor was harder than he'd imagined. He laid his hand on Sam's shoulder. "Take good care of her, son." Then he walked home.

Sam and Barbara stood in their front yard, watching their boys climb on the tractor.

"We can't have a tractor in our front yard," Barbara said.

"You said I needed a hobby."

"I was thinking of stamp collecting."

"You should have been more specific."

The tractor is still there, out front of their house underneath the oak trees. Sam and Barbara sit on their porch at night, looking at it. It's starting to grow on them.

"I don't care for marigolds," Barbara said one evening. "But I do think white geraniums would look nice up against the red."

The Corn and Sausage Days parade is three months away, and Sam has been asked to take part. He's thinking it over. The boys want him to. They want to ride on his lap and wave and throw candy.

Charlie's excited at the prospect. He said to Sam, "Come on, son. Ride in the parade. Take the boys along. You'll enjoy it."

He hopes Sam will do it. Legacies are hard to come by, after all. And if you have one going, you ought to do what you can to keep it alive.

Seven

The Date

Wayne Fleming and Deena Morrison have been attending church for two months. They sit in the former Wilbur Matthews pew, behind Fern Hampton. The meetinghouse isn't air-conditioned. If you look closely at the pew, you can see Wilbur's sweat outline. He's been dead thirty years, but remnants of his perspiration linger on.

Their first Sunday at worship, Wayne's three children sat between them. But over the past two months, Wayne and Deena have shuffled the children to the pew ends and are now sitting side by side. Sometimes their hips touch, which causes Wayne to think of things other than the Lord.

In the silence, when the Quakers sit with their heads bowed and their eyes closed, Wayne glances at Deena out of the corner of his right eye. It gives him a headache to stare sideways for such a long time, but to gaze at such loveliness makes the pain worthwhile.

The pew had sat empty since Wilbur died. People aren't accustomed to seeing anyone there. It doesn't feel right. Though they are happy for Wayne and Deena, they wish the couple had sat somewhere else out of respect for Wilbur's memory.

Their first Sunday there, Fern Hampton turned and said, "You know, the view from that pew isn't all that great. Why don't you sit somewhere else?"

Harmony Friends Meeting is not a user-friendly church. When Sam held an all-church workshop on how to make visitors feel welcome, not many people showed up. The ones who did argued with him.

The workshop was held in the basement. He had purchased the workshop materials from the Church Growth Institute of Valley Vista, California, after reading their ad in a ministers' magazine:

"Our church attendance tripled in six months. We're building a new sanctuary and fielding two new softball teams!"
— *The Reverend C.G., Georgia*

"Our offerings doubled in three weeks!!"
— *Pastor M.K., Iowa*

Sam's first proposal had been to reserve rows four through seven for visitors. "The rest of us can share pews. We don't all need our own pew. Let's not make our visitors sit in the front row."

"I've sat in the sixth row since I was a child," Fern Hampton said, verging on tears. "And now you're going to throw me out after all I've done for this church. That's the thanks I get? I'm glad my mother isn't alive to see this."

There were other concerns. Dale Hinshaw believed that telling the visitors where they should sit was a violation of their constitutional rights. "We can't be telling people where to sit. This is a free country. We oughta let them sit where they want to sit. The last thing we need is a lawsuit on our hands. No, sir, I don't think we oughta be telling people where to sit."

Sam tried to get his money back from the Church Growth Institute of Valley Vista, California, but they'd moved and had not left a forwarding address.

Deena talked over matters with Sam at the Legal Grounds Coffee Shop.

"Have Wayne and I made Fern Hampton mad?" she asked. "For some reason she doesn't want us sitting behind her. Are we not welcome?"

Sam sighed. "Just ignore her. Folks at church are just a little set in their ways, that's all."

"Set in their ways" is putting it mildly.

81

The church has used the same hymnals since 1943. They're held together with duct tape. Once Sam had suggested buying new hymnals, and they'd brought it up in his annual review in the "Areas Needing Improvement" section.

Shows a callous disregard for our religious tradition, the review read.

On another occasion, when Sam tried to move the offering from the front of the worship to the back, it became the subject of an all-church meeting. The meeting ended with Dale Hinshaw asking Sam whether he believed in the virgin birth.

"What's the virgin birth got to do with moving the offering?" Sam asked.

"Well, if you can't see it, then it's not for me to explain," Dale replied, clearly troubled.

But Deena and Wayne are sticking with it. They're there every Sunday, in the Wilbur Matthews pew with Wayne's three children.

Sunday is Wayne's favorite day of the week. It's his day to hope, his day to believe anything can happen. He sits in the pew and listens to the stories of old and prays for God to do something miraculous in his life.

He feels guilty asking God for anything while sitting in church with a woman he isn't married to. Sometimes when their hips are touching, the stirrings unsettle him and he'll slide away. Deena notices but isn't sure what to make of it.

Wayne puzzles her. All the other men she ever dated had one thing on their minds. But not Wayne. Though she appreciates his manners, she does wonder just how much he likes her. It's hard for her to tell. They've held hands, but that's it. He's never even tried to kiss her. One evening, he walked her home after she closed the shop. She waited for him to kiss her good-bye, but he shook her hand instead.

She talked about it with her grandmother over supper.

"Maybe he's gay," she told her grand-mother. "Maybe that's why his wife left."

"Don't be silly," Mabel Morrison said. "He's just bashful. You know, Deena, you don't have to sit around waiting for him to ask you out. Nowadays women ask men out. If you want to go on a date with Wayne Fleming, ask him."

The next evening, Wayne stopped past the Legal Grounds on his way to work. It was closing time. Deena flipped the sign on the door from *Open* to *Closed*. She poured Wayne a cup of coffee, and they sat at the table in the corner. She was wearing a new dress. She arranged herself in the chair across from Wayne, the picture of feminine charm.

"Would you like to go on a picnic this Saturday?" she asked. "I'll close the shop and we can go on a picnic."

"That would be fun. The kids would like that."

"Actually, I was hoping we could go by ourselves. My grandma can watch the kids."

Wayne hesitated. "I don't know. I am still married, after all. I mean, church is one thing, but a picnic with just the two of us, well, I'll need to think about that."

"Look, Wayne, your wife's been gone over a year now. She's not coming back. Wake up and smell the coffee. You need to get on with your life. Are you taking me on a picnic this Saturday or not? If you're not, I'm asking Ernie Matthews."

Ernie Matthews! Ernie Matthews had spent eight years in high school. Ernie Matthews wore his pants low. When he bent over, you could see the pale suggestion of a crevice.

"You'd really ask Ernie Matthews out?" Wayne asked.

"Watch me. And what's more, I'll tell everyone I turned you down for Ernie Matthews."

"Can we take roast beef sandwiches on the picnic?"

"Sure. Pack whatever you want," Deena said.

They laughed. Deena reached across the table and took Wayne's hand. "I'm looking forward to being alone with you," she said. Then she smiled.

Wayne blushed. His heart swam. Deena leaned forward.

Oh my, she wants a kiss, he thought.

He leaned forward. It was a wide table, and he couldn't quite reach her. He leaned further forward and knocked his mostly full coffee cup over onto Deena.

Wayne had given considerable thought to what their first kiss might be like, but had never contemplated this scenario.

"Daggonit, Deena, I'm sorry. Here, let me help you." He jumped to his feet and ran to get paper towels. He mopped the floor while she dabbed the coffee off her dress. They wiped off the table together. He looked at her. She looked at him.

"Let's try that again," Wayne said, and then he kissed Deena Morrison flush on her plump lips, just like Rhett Butler kissed Scarlet O'Hara in *Gone with the Wind*.

"My," Deena Morrison exclaimed. "My, oh my."

Wayne grinned a rakish grin, then said, "I'll pick you up at ten o'clock Saturday morning. Be ready."

Deena walked him to the door. She thought of kissing him again, but didn't want to seem overeager, so she squeezed his hand instead. After he left, she washed the coffee pots, turned off the lights, locked the doors, and walked home to her grandmother's house. Her grandmother was sitting in her chair in the living room, reading a book. She looked up as Deena came through the door.

"How'd it go?" she asked.

"He kissed me."

"Where?"

"In the coffee shop."

"No, I mean was it a peck on the cheek or a kiss on your lips?"

"My lips."

"Well, I guess that means he isn't gay."

That Saturday morning — a beautiful July morning, not too hot, not too sticky, just right — Wayne and his three kids pulled up to the curb in front of Mabel Morrison's home. Mabel and Deena were watching from the front window as they climbed from the truck.

"Say, he's a looker," Mabel said. "I've half a mind to go on that picnic and leave you here with the kids."

"Stay away from him, Grandma. He's mine."

"Since your father's not here, I think it's my job to lay down the law to this Wayne Fleming character."

The doorbell rang. Mabel opened the door and peered at Wayne. "Just what are your intentions with my favorite grand-daughter?"

Deena stood behind her, chuckling.

"I'm flying her to Las Vegas for a quickie wedding. Then we'll move in with you and have six children in five years. But don't worry about money. I'll apply for welfare, and with nine kids we'll make a bundle. Is that all right with you?"

"So long as you pick up your children by seven o'clock tonight so I can make my bridge club." Mabel bent down to the chil-dren and took their hands, "Come on, kids, your daddy and Deena have a plane to catch."

She hugged Deena good-bye. "Enjoy your picnic," she said. Then she whis-pered in Deena's ear, "I like him. I like him a lot."

Wayne and Deena walked to the truck.

"I like your grandmother," he said.

"Are we really going to Las Vegas to get

married?"

"Let's see how the picnic goes."

They drove through the country, past farms and fields and woods to a state park. His hand rested on the seat beside him. After a time, Deena reached over and took it. His insides shuddered. They parked the truck and hiked through the woods to a meadow. Wayne carried the picnic hamper with one hand and held Deena's hand with the other. They walked through the grass to a rise above a stream. Wayne spread the blanket on the ground. They ate lunch, then lay on their backs, side by side, looking up at the blue sky and talking.

They talked about everything. About their families and where they'd grown up. She told him about law school, and he told her about the classes he was taking to be a teacher.

Then they turned on their sides and looked at one another. He placed his hand gently upon her face, ready to pull it back in case she frowned. But she didn't frown; she smiled.

It had been a long time since he had whispered intimacies to a woman. He was a little out of practice.

"I hope you liked the sandwiches," he said.

"Oh, they were fine. It was nice of you to bring them."

"I had the lady at the deli make them." He stared at her a bit longer, then swallowed and took a deep breath. "You're a beautiful woman, Deena Morrison."

"You're a kind man, Wayne Fleming."

They lay side by side on the blanket, talking and watching the sky for the longest time.

When Deena was fourteen she'd written in her diary about the perfect date. It had taken eleven years, but now she'd finally had it.

They pulled up to Mabel Morrison's house a little before seven. Mabel left for bridge and Wayne and Deena sat on the porch talking while the children played tag in the front yard. Then five-year-old Kate settled into Deena's lap and fell asleep.

A little after nine, Wayne stood to leave. "Time I got the kids home," he said.

He carried Kate to the truck and propped her in the seat. Adam and Rachel squeezed in around her. Wayne buckled them in.

He climbed in the truck. Deena was standing at his door.

"Thank you," she said. "Can we go out again? Soon."

He smiled. He felt bold. "Only if we end up in Las Vegas."

Deena blushed.

He drove home in a fog of love. He ran the kids through the bathtub, brushed their teeth, tucked them in bed, and read them a story. He watched them as they fell asleep, three little breathing lumps lying in a row.

He went outside and sat on the front steps. He thought about Deena and their day together. He wished she were here now. Right beside him. For the rest of his life.

The phone rang through the screen door, an intrusion of noise. He hurried inside and picked it up. He could hear slight weeping on the other end.

"Hello," Wayne said. "Hello, who is this?"

"It's me, Wayne. Sally. Your wife. I want to come home. I want to be with you and the kids. I want us to be a family again. I'm so sorry. Will you take me back?"

Eight

The Jackpot

It never pays to ask if things can get worse, Jessie Peacock told herself on the way home from church.

It was the first Sunday in August. Asa was working overtime at the poultry plant, so she'd gone to church by herself. Vernley Stout, the bank president, had stopped Jessie on the steps outside the meeting-house.

"Jessie, I've done all I can, but the board's leaning on me pretty heavy. If you don't pay off last year's note, they're gonna put a lien against your farm. They want two thousand dollars by Friday."

Jessie lay awake all that night, wondering how to get the money. The only thing she had of any worth was her grandmother's quilts. Her mother had given them to Jessie just before she'd died. Ten hand-stitched quilts. She'd made Jessie promise to keep them in the family.

The next morning Jessie told Asa she needed the truck to visit her cousin. While he was working on the barn, she carried the quilts to the truck, drove to an antique store in the city, and sold them for two thousand dollars. Then she went to the bank and gave Vernley Stout the money.

"I'm glad you got the money," he told her. "I'm sorry I had to hurry you along, but I couldn't put off the board any longer."

"I don't blame you. You're just doing your job."

Vernley paused, then said, "Jessie, I'm not aiming to badger you, but you and Asa haven't put anything toward this year's note. Are you going to be able to pay that off when it comes due this fall? Tell me now, so I can maybe hold off the board."

"I don't know, Vernley, what with this drought and all. Asa's been working overtime at the poultry plant. We hope to have the money, but I can't say for sure."

The next day a registered letter from the state lottery office came just as Jessie was making lunch. Their mailman, Clarence, brought it to the back screen door and waited while Jessie signed for it. Clarence was curious about the envelope and hoped Jessie would open it while he was there, but she didn't. She thanked him, then closed the screen door, and sat at the kitchen table.

She opened the envelope and read:

This is to notify you that your winning lottery ticket will expire on August 23. If you do not accept your winnings by that date, you will forfeit any and all claims to the money.

There was a number to call at the bottom of the page.

Jessie thought about the note coming due. She rose from her chair and walked to the phone next to the refrigerator. She dialed the number. The phone rang and rang. Just as someone picked it up and said "State lottery office," she heard Asa crunching up the gravel lane in their truck.

"Oh, I must have misdialed. I'm sorry," Jessie said, and hung up the phone. She hid the letter underneath her mother's punch bowl on top of the refrigerator.

She and Asa ate baloney sandwiches at the kitchen table. They'd been eating a lot of baloney sandwiches lately.

He finished his lunch and went outside to work on the barn. Their Amish neighbor, Erven Schwartz, was helping Asa.

Jessie waited until she could hear their hammering, then picked up the phone and dialed the state lottery office. A woman answered the phone on the second ring.

Jessie told her her name.

"Say, I know you," the woman said. "You're the lady who turned down the money?"

"Yeah, well, I guess I'll be wanting that money after all." Jessie told her all that had happened, about the drought and their barn burning and the note coming due. She even told about selling her grandmother's quilts. She began to cry as she thought of the quilts. She felt stupid, crying to a stranger on the phone.

"Honey, maybe this is the Lord's way of helping you."

Jessie sniffed. "You think so?"

"Yes, I do. I don't think you should feel bad at all."

"What do I need to do to get the money?"

She heard the woman striking the keys on her computer.

"Well, honey, we can send you a little over twenty thousand dollars a month for the next twenty years or you can take a lump sum payment of three and a half million dollars. What do you want to do?"

The numbers staggered Jessie. She reached in her purse, pulled out a nickel, and tossed it in the air.

Heads.

"I'll take the three and a half million."

"It'll take a few days. We have to process

the check, then send it registered mail. You'll have it in two or three days, honey."

Clarence came that Friday just before lunch. Two registered letters in the space of a week. He was beside himself with curiosity.

"How are you, Clarence?"

"Oh, same old same old. How about you? Anything interesting happening?"

Jessie looked at the envelope. It was bowed out from where Clarence had looked through the little window to see what was inside.

"Nothing much happening here," she told him. "But if something does come up, I'll be sure to let you know."

She closed the door, sat down at the kitchen table, opened the envelope, and pulled out the check.

Pay to the order of Jessie Peacock, it read. *$3,500,000.* Then, on the line below that, *Three million, five hundred thousand dollars and no cents.*

She heard Asa's truck come up the lane, crunching the gravel. She put the check back in the envelope and hid it on top of the refrigerator under her mother's punch bowl.

They ate their lunch, then did their work. That evening she made Spam kabobs,

95

Asa's favorite dinner.

"Wow! Spam kabobs! What's the occasion?" he asked.

"No certain reason. I just wanted to make them for you."

It was Asa's night off from the poultry plant, so they washed the dishes together, standing at the sink, looking out the window. Then they sat on the porch. They could hear the frogs down at the creek.

Asa was quiet.

"What are you thinking, honey?" Jessie asked.

"I was just thinking to myself how many times I've sat on this porch worrying about my problems, and now I can't even remember most of what I worried about. The Lord sure has taken good care of us — providing me that job just when we needed the money, having Erven help me with the barn. The Lord sure has taken good care of us."

"He certainly has." Jessie thought of the check in the kitchen underneath her mother's punch bowl. Her thirty pieces of silver.

She wanted to tell him about the money, but was too ashamed. He'd been so proud of her when she'd turned down the money. She wondered if she could spend the money without Asa's knowing it. Maybe put it in the bank in the next town over and draw out a little at a time. Just enough to pay the bills.

She was wondering about that when Asa stood up and said, "Let's turn on the news and see what's going on in the world."

He pushed open the wooden screen door, walked into the front room, and arranged himself in his recliner. Jessie sat next to him in her chair.

He turned on Channel 5, just in time to hear the anchorman say, "A local woman is three and a half million dollars richer today. We'll tell you more after this commercial break."

"Wow," Asa said. "Think of that. Three and a half million dollars. Of course, all the money in the world won't bring a man peace of mind."

Jessie stood up and said, "Did you hear that?"

"Hear what?" He turned off the television set.

"The chickens. I think I hear the chickens. I wonder if there's a fox in the chicken coop again?"

Asa bolted from his chair and ran out the kitchen door toward the coop.

Jessie hurried behind the television, unplugged the antenna, then went outside.

"Is everything all right?" she yelled from the porch.

"A-okay!" Asa yelled back from the coop.

They returned to the house. Asa settled back in his chair and pushed the ON button. The television was snowy white.

"Now what's the matter?" he said.

"I think it's broken. It's been acting up lately."

"Rats! I wanted to see who won all that money."

"Probably no one we know."

The phone rang in the kitchen.

"Now who'd be calling this late at night?" Asa wondered aloud.

Jessie hurried to answer it. It was Dale Hinshaw.

"Say, Jessie, they was just talking about you on the TV. I thought you'd turned that money down. Speaking of money, I'd like to talk with you about my Scripture egg project. I just felt the Lord leading me to ask if you want to donate a little something toward it. Can I stop by your house to-morrow morning?"

"I can't talk now," Jessie said, and hung up the phone. She took the phone off the hook and placed it on the counter.

"Who was that?" Asa called from the front room.

"A man selling aluminum siding."

It was late. They went upstairs and got ready for bed. By the time Jessie worked up her courage to tell Asa about the money, he was almost asleep. She said in a quiet voice, "Asa?"

It was dark in their bedroom. She could feel him shift toward her.

"Yes."

"I've done something I need to tell you about."

"What is it, honey?"

"Remember those letters we've been getting from the lottery people?"

"Uh-huh."

"Well, I called them up and talked with the nicest lady. And, well, I just got to thinking how this might be the Lord's way of taking care of us and, well, I went ahead and took the money."

Asa came wide awake. He sat up and turned on the lamp beside their bed.

"We have five million dollars?"

"Actually, only three and a half million. I picked the instant payment over the twenty-year payout."

"When do we get the money?"

"The check came today. It's downstairs."

"Can I see it?"

They climbed from the bed, pulled their robes from the bedposts, and walked down the stairs.

Jessie reached up under the punch bowl and pulled the check out. They sat at the kitchen table, across from one another.

Asa peered at the check. He held it up to the light. "It looks real," he said.

"Oh, it's real. Clarence brought it in the registered mail."

"It makes me kind of nervous, having all this money in the house." He walked over to the kitchen door and locked it.

"Let's take it to the bank first thing in the morning," Jessie said.

"Does that mean we're going to keep it?"

Jessie grew quiet, then reached across the table and took his hand.

"Asa, don't take this wrong — you've taken good care of me over the years. But lately it's been kind of tough. It's wearing me out. Maybe if we could just pay off our bills and set aside some money for when we get old, we could give the rest away. Maybe give it to the church or something."

"I've been trying my best to keep our heads above water."

"I'm not blaming you. The pigs died, and we've had this drought. It couldn't be helped. But now we can get ahead. We can

100

finish that new barn and buy some more livestock and pay off our debt." She didn't tell him about selling her grandmother's quilts.

"Maybe this is the Lord's way of taking care of us," Asa agreed. "We've been praying for help. Maybe this is the answer."

They put the check back underneath the punch bowl and went upstairs to bed.

Asa pulled Jessie close. "I've never slept with a millionaire before," he said. She laughed. It was music to him. She hadn't laughed in a long time.

"You know," Asa said, "if we did keep it, we could do some real good with this money. We could help a lot of people."

"That's what I've been thinking."

They woke up next morning, ate breakfast, and went to the bank. Vernley Stout waved as they walked through the doors.

"They talked about you last night on the television," he said to Jessie. "I think I know why you're here."

"We want to pay off the notes," Asa said.

"Well, you just have the one now."

"I don't think so. I believe we still owe two thousand dollars on last year's note."

Vernley Stout looked at Jessie, perplexed.

Jessie began to weep. "I paid it off. I sold my grandmother's quilts while you were at work one day. They were gonna put a lien against us. I had to do it."

Vernley said, "It couldn't be helped, Asa. I tried to talk the board out of it, but they wouldn't listen. They wanted their money."

"Your grandmother's quilts?" Asa asked Jessie. "The ones your mother gave you?"

Jessie sniffed and nodded.

They deposited the check and paid off the note. Then Asa drew out four thousand dollars in cash.

"What's that for?" Jessie asked.

"You'll see soon enough."

They climbed into the truck. Asa turned to Jessie. "Who'd you sell the quilts to?"

She told him. He eased the truck into gear and drove toward the city. Two hours later they pulled up to the shop and went inside.

Jessie's quilts were displayed throughout the shop. Asa counted nine.

"My wife sold you ten quilts. What happened to the other one?" he asked the lady behind the counter.

"I sold the wedding ring quilt."

That had been the oldest quilt, given to Jessie's grandmother on her wedding day. Jessie blinked back tears.

"I'd like to buy all the quilts," Asa told the lady.

It took the whole four thousand dollars. They had just enough money left for lunch. They turned into their lane in early afternoon, carried the quilts upstairs, and stored them in the chest. As they closed the lid on the trunk, Asa drew Jessie to him. "Don't ever do that again," he told her. "We can't afford to buy them back again, even if we are millionaires."

They did their chores. By then, it was time for supper. They ate leftover Spam kabobs from the night before.

"I'll bet no millionaire is eating better than we are tonight," Asa said. "Could you pass me another kabob, please?"

They washed the dishes and then sat on the porch, rocking back and forth, talking about their day.

"I'm bushed," Jessie said. "It's hard work being rich."

After a time they went in the house, turned off the downstairs lights, brushed their teeth, and went to bed.

Asa held Jessie to him in the dark.

"I'm sorry about your grandmother's wedding ring quilt. If you want, I'll try to find out who bought it and get it back for you."

"That's okay. That's what I get for my foolishness. I just hope whoever has it appreciates it."

She tried not to cry, thinking about it. It's an odd thing, how every blessing has its shadow. Their bills were paid. They had more money than they knew what to do with. But at that moment Jessie would have paid a million dollars to have her grandma's quilt back.

She didn't say that to Asa. She just wiggled into him and said, "I love you, honey."

"I love you back."

He reached up and turned off the light above the bed and fell asleep.

Jessie eased the covers off and stole over to the blanket chest. She took one of her grandmother's quilts and spread it on the bed, then got underneath the covers. Smelling the quilt and the memories behind it, she went to sleep.

Nine

A Dubious Blessing

Jessie Peacock was glad she'd told Asa about accepting the lottery money, especially since it was the headline story in that week's edition of the *Harmony Herald*. When they went to church that Sunday and the offering plate drew near their row, Bea Majors stopped playing the organ, raised off her seat, and peered at Asa to see if he would give anything. All across the meeting room, people were watching.

The offering plate stopped at row six while Fern Hampton fumbled in her purse for two dollars. Then it was passed to the Wayne Fleming and Deena Morrison pew, formerly the Wilbur Matthews pew. Deena dropped her offering in the plate, then handed it to Dale Hinshaw, the morning's usher, who executed a well-rehearsed backward full step with a half turn to row eight — the Jessie and Asa Peacock pew.

Wayne and Deena hadn't read the *Herald*. They couldn't figure out why everyone was staring at them. Then Fern Hampton whispered, "Hey, you're blocking my view. Slide over," and that's when they realized people were looking at Jessie and Asa, not them.

Wayne slid over and turned to watch, just as Asa eased a check from his billfold, placed it in the offering, and passed the plate to Dale. Dale plucked the check from the plate, unfolded it, and read the numbers.

"Yep, they tithed. Three hundred and fifty thousand dollars," he announced to the congregation.

Bea Majors resumed her playing, but no one was listening. They were turned in their pews, talking to one another.

"Seems they could have given a little more, what with all the money they won," Fern Hampton commented to Charlie and Gloria Gardner.

"Maybe this means we can get some uniforms for our new basketball team," Bill Muldock whispered to his brother, Harvey.

Dale Hinshaw was thinking to himself: If I had twenty thousand of that, I could take the Scripture egg project international. Maybe even ship some eggs to the Muslims. His mind reeled at the possibilities.

He and Ellis Hodge made their way down front with the offering and stood in front of the pulpit.

"Let us pray," Sam Gardner said. People stopped talking and bowed their heads. Bea Majors softened her organ playing. Lately, she'd been playing the organ while Sam prayed. She'd gotten the idea from watching a TV preacher. Sam didn't care for it, but she was the only person in the church who knew how to play the organ so she was beyond correction. Occasionally, while Sam was preaching, she would play background music for emphasis.

"Lord, we thank you for all the gifts you've given us. May we use them for your glory," Sam prayed, while Bea played "We Give Thee but Thine Own."

"Amen," said the congregation, and worship was over.

Sam gathered up his sermon notes and tucked them in his Bible. Seventy-seven down, one thousand four hundred and twenty-three sermons to go, he thought. He had twenty-nine years left on a thirty-year mortgage. He'd counted up all the sermons he'd have to preach before his mortgage was paid off. Fifty sermons a year for thirty years equaled fifteen hundred sermons. He'd be sixty-nine years old. He had doubts about whether he'd make it.

What began as discouragement for Sam in April had by June moved into depression and was now, in mid-August, full-fledged unbelief.

These people would cause Jesus to become an atheist, Sam told himself.

The tractor hadn't helped. It was just one more pressure. One more thing to take care of.

As it was, Sam had plenty enough worries. Giving had been down at church. People would drop a dollar in the plate, thinking that would do it. The chairmen of the committees would spend money the church didn't have. Sam would point out that they didn't have the money.

"Well, it's right there in the budget," they'd say. "It says right there on line twelve that our committee has eight hundred dollars to spend."

"But if people aren't giving money, then we don't have it to spend, no matter what line twelve says," Sam would explain.

"Well, I never heard of such a thing. Pastor Taylor never said anything like that. He never talked about money."

Which is why our church is down to ninety-five dollars and my last three paychecks have been late, Sam wanted to say.

He'd been thinking of taking a part-time job, in case the church had to cut his pay. A friend from seminary had become a salesman for the Eternal Life Insurance Company of Colorado Springs, Colorado. He'd called Sam the month before, long distance from the city, to ask Sam if he wanted to sell life insurance.

"You can stay right there in Harmony and be a pastor. In fact, most of our agents are pastors. We'll send you to school in Colorado for two weeks at our expense. You could pull in another twenty thousand dollars a year, maybe more. How about it?"

Sam told him he'd think about it. He could use the money but wasn't sure he had the time. He had only one day off a week as it was. Hardly saw his boys. They might as well not even have a father, for all the time he saw them.

So when Asa and Jessie Peacock tithed their lottery winnings, Sam was greatly relieved. Maybe the church could pay him on time now. Maybe they'd even give him a raise and more time with his family.

Sam speculated about it at his parents' house that Sunday afternoon. He and Barbara were sitting with his parents on their porch after dinner.

"This is sure good news for the church," Sam said. "We can invest that money. The interest alone would pay my salary. Just think, I'd always get paid on time."

"Don't count on that happening," Charlie Gardner said. "It would make too much sense. I remember, it was about twenty years ago, when Bea and Opal's mother died and left eighty thousand dollars to the church. That was some serious money, let me tell you."

"We had eighty thousand dollars? I never heard anything about it," Sam said.

"Yeah, well, it's still a sore point. People don't talk about it much. We were gonna build on to the meetinghouse, so the trustees hired some fancy architect from the city to draw up the plans and that cost sixty thousand dollars and there went our money. We had twenty thousand left, which the trustees used to put a new roof on the meetinghouse. It was a special kind of roof, guaranteed for life."

"But our meetinghouse roof leaks like a sieve."

"Yeah, the company that did it went out of business."

"Well, I'm sure people have learned a lesson and won't let this money go to waste," Barbara said.

Charlie peered at Sam's wife. "These are the same people who think Dale Hinshaw's Scripture eggs are a good idea."

"We're sunk," Sam said.

"Doomed," added his mother.

"You watch and see," Charlie Gardner said. "That money will burn a hole in their pockets."

They sat on the porch, glum.

That Thursday was the third Thursday of the month, the night of the monthly elders meeting. They gathered down in the basement of the meetinghouse at the folding table next to the noodle freezer.

They were all on time for once. Miriam Hodge opened with a prayer, then steered their way in record time through the reading of the minutes and the old business.

"Is there any new business?" she asked the elders.

"I'd like to propose the church donate twenty thousand dollars to the Scripture egg project," Dale Hinshaw said. "I think we can reach the Muslims in a big way."

Dale had a globe with him, with straight pins stuck on fifty cities throughout the Middle East, Asia, and Africa.

"These are your major Muslim strongholds," he continued. "If we could hand out ten thousand Scripture eggs a year in those cities, we could do some serious damage for the Kingdom. I've figured out a way we can do it using missionaries already in place. We

111

could mail one hundred chickens to each missionary."

"Excuse me," Miriam said, "but don't those people speak different languages?"

"I've already thought of that. The missus is home right now working on the translations. She's having a little trouble with Swahili, but she'll make it."

"I'm not sure the church would approve spending twenty thousand dollars in such a way," Miriam said.

"Well, I'd hate to think the day has come when we've lost our heart for the lost."

"Supposing we could give you ten thousand? What could you do with that?" Harvey Muldock asked.

"Well, I suppose we could send maybe fifty chickens to each missionary. Of course, that'll slow the spread of God's Word. So long as you're willing to stand before the Almighty and justify your actions, I guess I could try it on ten thousand."

"I approve giving Dale ten thousand dollars for the Scripture egg project," Harvey proposed, unfazed at the prospect of standing before the Almighty.

"Does this meet with your approval?" Miriam asked the other elders.

"Approved," they rumbled, except for Asa Peacock. He just sat in his chair, thinking. Ten thousand dollars for Scripture eggs. This wasn't what he and Jessie had in mind when they'd given the money to the church.

They'd talked about it that morning at the breakfast table.

"Wouldn't it be wonderful if Wayne Fleming could get his diploma and land a decent job and buy a house for those kids? Maybe the church could give some of the money to him," Jessie had said. "Why don't you propose that at tonight's meeting?"

"Now there's a fine idea," Asa had agreed.

So when Miriam asked, "Is there any other new business?" Asa raised his hand.

"Well, Jessie and I were talking this morning and we were thinking how nice it could be if the church could maybe help Wayne Fleming. He's been working nights at the Kroger and taking one class at a time. Maybe we could give him enough money so's he could work part-time and finish college, and then . . ."

Fern Hampton interrupted, "Are he and that Deena living together?"

"Most certainly not," Sam Gardner said. "She's living with her grandmother."

"Still, I don't think it's right that they come to church together," Fern said. "Him

113

being married and all. And I don't think they ought to sit in Wilbur Matthews's pew like that."

"Fern, Wilbur's been dead for twenty-five years," Sam said.

"I still think they could be more respectful of his memory."

"I think it's wonderful they're coming to church and I hope it works out for them to get married," Miriam said. "Those children need a mother."

She turned to Asa. "I think your idea is a fine one. Why don't we approach Wayne and see how much money he'd need to cut his work hours and take more classes?"

"I'd be happy to talk with Wayne," Sam said.

"Now hold your horses," Harvey said. "I believe we're starting a dangerous precedent here. What happens the next time someone else needs help? We oughta think long and hard before just jumping in and helping someone like that."

"We'd be encouraging adultery," Fern said.

"Far be it for me to judge, but I think Fern's right," Dale said.

Sam sighed. For a fleeting moment, he'd believed the church was going to do something worthwhile. He'd felt a momentary rise of hope. I should have known better, he thought.

Harvey cleared his throat. "As long as we're on the subject of money, my brother Bill is requesting a thousand dollars for uniforms and shoes for the church basketball team. And we figured that as long as we're gonna have new uniforms we maybe should build a new gymnasium onto the meetinghouse." He passed some papers to Dale, sitting on his left. "Take one of these, Dale, and pass 'em down."

"We've worked up some figures. If we do some of the labor ourselves, painting and such, we can build a gymnasium off the west end of the meetinghouse for a little under three hundred and forty thousand, which is just what we have left. Now if that ain't a sign from the Lord, I don't know what is. Of course, it just wouldn't be for the basketball team. We could use it for other things too — the Chicken Noodle Dinner, the ladies' quilt project, revivals, emergency housing during national catastrophes. What do you think?"

"I tell you one thing," Fern said. "I'm not sure how much longer the ladies can keep making noodles down in the basement, what with all those stairs. Our knees can barely take it. Speaking on behalf of the

Friendly Women's Circle, I think it's a wonderful idea."

"Let's discuss this a little further," Miriam said. "That's an awful lot of money for something we really don't need."

"I think Miriam's right. We don't need a gymnasium," said Sam.

"I disagree," Dale said. "If we had a gymnasium we could have a Bible aerobics class like that new church in town."

"That would certainly help our knees," Fern pointed out.

"I think the Lord's will on this is becoming pretty clear," Harvey said. "Does everyone else approve?"

"Approved," rumbled the elders, except for Sam, Miriam, and Asa.

Asa was sorry he and Jessie had donated the money. A gymnasium, he thought. What in thunder will we do with a gymnasium?

Sam looked at his watch. He thought to himself, It took us thirty minutes to spend three hundred and fifty thousand dollars. That's got to be a record.

"I'd like to make a proposal," Fern said. "As most of you know, my mother was a sainted member of this church all her life." She paused and sniffed and dabbed her eyes with a Kleenex. "I think it's only fitting that we name our new building in honor of her. The Fleeta Hampton Memorial Gymnasium. And I won't even ask if the rest of you approve, because I know you do."

They should have seen it coming. It was just like Fern Hampton to not put a dime toward something, then have it named for someone in her family. There was the Fred Hampton Memorial Drinking Fountain and the Frieda Hampton Memorial Crib, which Frank the secretary had bought for the Iverson Chinese twins. Fern had gone and had a plaque made with her sister's name on it and had bolted it right to the crib. The thing of it was, Frieda Hampton hadn't even liked children, and children hadn't liked her.

This is it, Sam thought. I'm selling insurance.

Miriam said, "I think this a misuse of Jessie and Asa's generous gift."

"Now, Miriam, don't be a sore loser," Dale said. "The Lord loves a cheerful loser. It says that in the Bible."

"Actually, it says the Lord loves a cheerful giver," Sam said.

"Sam, you shouldn't misquote Scripture just to get your way," Dale said.

If I quit now, Sam thought, I could be selling insurance in two weeks. Maybe my folks could loan me a little money to tide us over.

That was the end of the meeting. Sam walked home. He was tired. More tired than he had ever been.

His thoughts ranged. What good is the church? What good does it do to even be faithful to God? It's not like God returns the favor. It's not like God actually causes people to do the right thing. It's not like I gave up on God. He gave up on me. Who needs Him? Not me, that's for sure.

Sam Gardner walked down Washington Street past the Grant Hardware Emporium. He stood outside his house. He could see Barbara through the upstairs window, combing their boys' hair after their bath.

I'll stick it out for them, he thought. But if a better offer comes along, I'm outta here.

He pushed open the door and went inside, up the stairs and into the bathroom. His boys were clustered in front of the mirror, brushing their teeth. Tanned, skinny boys in their Superman underwear and burr haircuts, frothing at the mouth. Rinse, spit, rinse, spit, and wipe.

"Daddy's home. Read us a story, Daddy. Read us a story."

It was the first time he'd seen them that day.

Starting now, I'm taking more time off. If folks in the church can be selfish, so can I.

He tucked his children in bed and read them a story as they fell asleep. He placed the book on the nightstand and pulled the sheets over their skinny shoulders. He stood between their beds, watching them, envying their innocence, their untainted hearts.

To fall asleep without a worry in the world, to trust as they trust — what a treasure that would be. Help me, Lord. Help me trust like them again.

Ten

A Hint of Hope

It had been a little over a month since Sally had called home. For weeks Wayne Fleming stewed about what to do. Finally, one morning in early September, he asked the neighbor lady to watch the kids while he went to talk with Sam Gardner.

He drove into town, parked behind the meetinghouse, and walked in through the back door. Frank the secretary was on the phone. He looked at Wayne, rolled his eyes, then covered the mouthpiece with his hand and told Wayne, "Be with you in a second."

"Take your time. I'm in no hurry."

Frank spoke into the phone. "Like I was saying, Fern, Sam isn't here. Monday's his day off. But I'll be sure to tell him you didn't like his sermon. Good-bye." He hung up the phone. "I woke up this morning with one nerve and darned if Fern Hampton didn't get on it."

"What's she complaining about now?"

"Oh, she claims Sam looked at her when he was talking about the Pharisees during his sermon yesterday morning. Now she's all upset."

"You would think she'd get the hint."

Frank laughed. "Yeah, wouldn't you, though."

"I heard you tell her today was Sam's day off. I was hoping to talk with him. I don't suppose I could talk with him today, could I?"

"Not today. Is there anything I can help you with?"

"I don't think so. It's kind of personal."

"Sit down, Wayne, and let's talk. You'll feel better getting it off your chest."

Wayne thought for a moment. "Maybe you're right. You've been married. Maybe you can help me." He sat in the chair beside Frank's desk. "Got a call from my wife. It's the first I've heard from her since she ran off with that truck driver last year. Now, out of the blue, she calls and wants to come home. I can't decide what to do."

"When did she call?"

"The first time was a month or so ago."

"I notice you've been spending time with Deena Morrison. Have you told her?"

"Not yet. But I'm aiming to just as soon as I get the chance. I thought I ought to make up my mind first about what I'm going to do."

"Which way are you leaning?"

"When Sally first called, I didn't want anything to do with her, and I told her so. Told her not to call me back. I didn't hear from her for a couple weeks. Then she called back the other night and we talked, and when I hung up I wasn't so sure anymore. She's coming home this Saturday to see the kids. She seems really sorry. I'm just not sure I can trust her anymore. I worry if I take her back, she'll cheat on me again."

"How do you know she cheated on you?"

"Well, that's what folks are saying, and I'm inclined to believe them."

Frank stood up, walked to the door, and closed it. Then he sat down, reached over to the phone, and took it off the hook.

"Wayne, I want to tell you something that happened to me a long time ago, when I was in Korea, back when Martha and I were first married. I need you to promise you'll never tell a soul."

"I won't say a word."

"I'd been over there about a year when I got a letter from her saying she wanted a divorce, that she'd fallen in love with someone else." Frank hesitated. His voice caught, remembering the pain of it. "Well, it was the worst day of my life, getting that letter. Forty-eight years ago, and it still hurts to think of it."

"I know that feeling," Wayne said quietly.

"I was due to be shipped home in three months. I wrote Martha a letter, asking her not to do anything until we'd talked. When I finally got home, she met me at the train station in the city. I could tell right off she'd been with another fella. Just by the way she looked at me. It liked to have killed me."

"There's no pain worse."

"I talked her into meeting with our pastor, and we were able to patch things up. But it was a lot of work, and it took a while."

"Why'd she cheat on you?"

"She never said. I asked her once, but she wouldn't say. I can't help but think she was lonely."

"But that's different. My wife wasn't lonely. I wasn't in Korea. I was home."

"Loneliness isn't about proximity. You can live with another person and still feel like there's no one who'll listen, like there's no one who cares. Anyway, my point is this — that after a time we worked it out, and in the end I was so grateful to God for letting me have my Martha. I don't know why she did what she did, but we rose above it, and so can you and Sally."

They sat quietly in the office. The Frieda Hampton Memorial Clock in the meeting room bonged ten.

"I have a lot of thinking to do," Wayne finally said.

"You sure do. I hope you make the right decision."

"I'd still like to talk with Sam. Can you ask him to call me tomorrow?"

"Sure."

"Thanks for talking with me, Frank. It means a lot."

"Take care of yourself, Wayne. I'll be thinking of you."

"I appreciate that."

Wayne thought about it all that day, and again that night as he swept the aisles at the Kroger. The next morning he woke up his children, read them a story, poured their bowls of Cap'n Crunch, and sat at the table with them.

"Kids, there's something you need to know. Your mommy will be coming home to visit us this Saturday."

They looked puzzled, then bombarded him with questions.

"Is Mommy coming back for good?"

"Can Deena still be our friend?"

"Does this mean Mommy loves us again?"

"Kids, I don't know quite what it means. But no matter what happens, I'll be here for you and I'll always take care of you. I want you to remember that."

The phone rang. Wayne picked it up.

"Hello."

"Hi, Wayne. This is Sam. Frank said you'd stopped by yesterday needing to talk. I'm free now. Can you come in?"

"Now's a bad time. I don't have a baby-sitter."

"I'd be happy to come to your place, if you want."

"That'd be great. I really need to talk."

"See you in a half hour then," Sam said, and hung up the phone.

Wayne looked around the trailer. It was a mess. He clapped his hands. "All right, kids, breakfast is over. Let's get things picked up." He filled the sink with soapsuds and handed Adam a dishcloth. "You're in charge of dishes, son."

The girls picked up the clutter while Wayne vacuumed. Little Kate yelled at him over the roar of the sweeper. "Can we stay up late when Mommy comes home?"

"We'll see," Wayne said.

He finished sweeping, wound the cord around the handle, and pushed the sweeper into the closet just as Sam Gardner knocked on the door.

"Come in," Wayne called out.

125

Sam pushed open the door and walked in the small trailer. Lord, what do they do on days when it rains? No wonder Sally ran off, Sam thought.

He and Wayne shook hands. Sam rubbed the kids' heads.

"Okay, kids, Daddy needs to talk with Sam. I need you to go outside to play. Be sure to stay back from the road."

Wayne sat on the couch. Sam sat opposite him in a saggy, green chair with worn armrests.

"We're so happy to have you and Deena and the kids coming to church," Sam said. "I take it things are going all right with the two of you?"

"Going really well. We enjoy each other's company." Wayne sighed, fidgeted on the sofa, then plunged ahead.

"My wife called last month and wants me to take her back. She's coming in this Saturday to see the kids and to talk with me. And I don't know what to do."

Sam leaned forward in his chair. "Wow, how did Deena take it?"

"The thing is, I haven't really gotten around to telling Deena yet."

"Well, it's none of my business, but don't you think you oughta tell her before Saturday?"

126

"Yeah, I suppose so." Wayne leaned forward and covered his face with his hands. "What a mess. Why did this have to happen? Deena and I were doing so well. Now everything's falling apart. Why couldn't Sally have stayed gone?"

Sam had taken several counseling classes in seminary, but his teachers had never covered this particular topic — what to do if your spouse runs off and you fall in love with a wonderful person only to have your spouse come home.

What a mess, Sam thought.

He'd been trained in the counseling classes never to tell people what to do. The key was to help people find the answers for themselves through skillful, insightful questioning. Sam had never been very good at it.

"Well, I tell you what I'd do," Sam said. "I'd forget about her. She abandoned you and the kids. Just walked off for no good reason. If that isn't a reason to divorce, I don't know what is."

"You think so? Frank told me I should take her back."

"He what?"

"He told me I should give Sally another chance. That I wouldn't regret it."

"When did he tell you that?"

"Yesterday at your office. You weren't

there, so I talked with Frank instead. Actually, what he said made a lot of sense."

Darn that Frank, Sam thought. That's what I get for taking a day off.

"Well, Wayne, you're free to talk with Frank or anyone else for that matter, but I'd advise keeping your own counsel. Everyone's gonna have a different idea of what you should do, and if you don't do what they suggest, they'll be mad."

"Yeah, you're probably right. It's just that I'm not sure what the right thing is. I've been praying about it, but God's not given me any kind of answer."

Good luck there, Sam thought. I've been asking God to do something in the church for over a year and nothing's happened.

"Why do you suppose God hasn't given me an answer?" Wayne asked.

"I'm not sure, Wayne."

"It makes it kind of hard to believe in God. If you know what I mean."

"I know exactly what you mean."

Sam suddenly felt very tired. He sagged in the green chair.

"Is anything wrong, Sam?"

"Hey, I'm not here to tell you my problems. I'm here to help you."

"I don't mind listening."

"Really?"

"Not at all. And I can keep a secret."

Sitting in that little trailer on the worn green chair, Sam felt like he was in a confessional. Safe and anonymous. Far away from Dale Hinshaw and Fern Hampton. Maybe it would be all right to tell Wayne his doubts.

He remembered back to when he was first called to the ministry, how he'd gone to Pastor Taylor to talk with him about being a pastor.

"There'll be times," Pastor Taylor had told Sam in a quiet, hesitant voice, "when your flock will minister to you. Dark nights of the soul when it feels you've lost your way. And you have to let them. Sam, you have to let them help you."

Sam was young then, brimming with the conviction of youth. He couldn't imagine such a time. He'd almost forgotten that long-ago conversation. Now it returned to his mind. He knew precisely what Pastor Taylor had been trying to say.

"It's like this, Wayne. Being a pastor and all, people expect me to have a strong faith, but here lately . . . well, here lately I've been struggling."

"Struggling? What do you mean by 'struggling'?"

"I mean there are times I'm sitting in church or preaching and it occurs to me that I don't believe in God anymore."

The moment Sam said it, he regretted it. His secret was out. There was no going back.

"How can you not believe in God?"

"I'm just not seeing Him do anything. Our Goal-Setting Sunday was a joke. People are always fighting with each other. Now we got all this money and the elders want to build a gymnasium onto the meetinghouse. And I'm not doing anybody a lick of good, either. I pray and pray for something to happen, for God to use me, for God to change the church, but nothing happens. Nothing at all."

"Have you told anyone? Have you talked with the elders?"

"Not a soul, except for you and my wife."

Wayne sat quietly on the couch for a moment. He could hear the children playing outside and the occasional hum of a passing car.

"Do you want my advice?" asked Wayne.

"Sure. I'm not promising I'll take it, but I'm curious to know your thoughts."

"I haven't been a Christian very long, but I've been reading the Bible you gave me. It talks a lot about honesty. Why don't you

130

just tell folks the truth about how you feel? Talk about it with the elders. Tell them your doubts. Maybe they can help you. Maybe they'll pray for you or something."

Sam laughed. "Yeah, they'll pray for me all right, right before they fire me."

"You don't know that."

"Well, I can't imagine they'd want to have a pastor who doesn't believe in God. I mean, belief in God is kind of in the job description."

"Still, I think it pays to be honest and up front."

"Boy, that's not easy."

"You got that right. Why do you think I haven't told Deena about my wife coming in this Saturday?"

"It looks like we both have some work ahead of us, doesn't it?"

Wayne nodded in agreement.

They talked about other things, about Asa and Jessie giving the money to the church, about Deena, about the Corn and Sausage Days festival the upcoming weekend.

Finally, Sam stood from the green chair. "Good luck talking with Deena."

"Good luck talking with the elders."

Sam walked toward the door, and Wayne followed.

"Hey, Sam, I know you don't think God's doing much in our little church, but I want you to know He's doing something in me. Even with all my troubles, I'm feeling a sense of hope I've never felt before. And I want you to know something else. Even though you think you're not doing any good, you've helped me more than you know."

He hugged Sam to him.

Sam's eyes burned. He squeezed Wayne back.

"Thank you, Wayne. Pray for me, could you?"

"You know I will."

Sam pushed open the trailer door, walked outside, climbed into his car, and drove past the fields and farms toward town. Past Harvey Muldock's car dealership. He pulled into town, passing beneath the Corn and Sausage Days banner strung across Main Street between Kivett's Five and Dime and the Kroger.

Kyle Weathers was out front of his barbershop, hanging up a sign. *Corn and Sausage Days Special! Haircuts While U Wait!*

Sam pulled the car behind the meetinghouse and walked inside. Frank looked up from his desk.

"How'd your visit go with Wayne?" he asked.

"Better than I'd hoped."

"Hope. Isn't that a lovely word?"

In his advancing years, Frank is softening. He's taken down the sign over his desk that read, *I Can Only Help One Person Each Day. Today Is Not Your Day. Tomorrow Doesn't Look Good Either.*

"It is a lovely word," Sam agreed.

"You know what Emily Dickinson said about hope, don't you?"

"It doesn't come to mind."

"She said, 'Hope is the thing with feathers that perches in the soul, and sings the tune without the words, and never stops at all.' "

"That's beautiful. What's it mean?"

"I'm not exactly certain. But I think it means that hope keeps singing its song. And even if we can't always hear it, it's still being sung."

Sam thought about that for a moment. "Yeah, I suppose you're right. I suppose that's precisely what it means."

Eleven

Jessie and Asa Come to Terms

Asa and Jessie Peacock hadn't realized being rich could be such a tribulation. They'd been wealthy only a month and a half and were already tired.

Vernley Stout from the bank had met with them to plan their investments. "The trick," Vernley explained, "is to let your money work for you."

Jessie was a little put out with Vernley. When they had opened their savings account twenty years ago, the bank had given them a free toaster, which was now on the blink. She had thought of buying a toaster, but had decided against it. "Let's wait and see what the bank will do," she'd told Asa.

She kept waiting for Vernley to say something about a new toaster, but he hadn't. Instead, he'd talked about mutual funds and annuities and other complexities Jessie and Asa didn't understand.

She began to drop hints to Vernley about wanting a new toaster.

"I sure could use a new toaster," she remarked one day in his office. "Ours is worn out. I heard the bank over in Cartersburg is giving a toaster away with every new account. And not a piddly two-slot toaster either. A four-slotter with a built-in bagel slicer."

But Vernley never took the hint.

Jessie wasn't accustomed to having all this money. She'd walk down the small-appliance aisle at Kivett's Five and Dime, studying the toasters. Reading the prices, she'd shake her head.

Maybe I can pick one up at a garage sale somewhere, she'd think.

It was the little things that threw her. Deciding to give her church three hundred and fifty thousand dollars came automatically. But spending thirty dollars on a toaster had preoccupied her for weeks.

She thought the money would ease her life, though that hadn't happened. She had been getting irate letters from an antigambling organization, the Network Against Gambling (NAG). When she'd first refused the lottery money, they'd written a story about her in the NAG newsletter. She had been the NAG poster child. But now that she'd accepted the money, the members of NAG were turning on her.

One day Clarence the mailman brought a

letter from a woman up north near Fort Wayne. Jessie sat at her kitchen table and read it.

> Your decision to refuse the money gave me such hope. I'd just become a Christian and your testimony was an inspiration to me, to think there were people like you out there in the world. When you changed your mind and took the money after all, I was devastated. I now wonder if I should even be a Christian. I just thought you should know.

I've caused a little one to stumble. Lord, forgive me, Jessie prayed.

She showed the letter to Asa.

"Well, all I can say is she must not have had much of a faith to start with," he said. "A person like that, they have a head cold and it causes them to question the Lord. Don't worry about it, Jessie — it's not your fault."

But she did worry about it. The newspaper from the city had carried a story about NAG falling on hard times. The president of NAG laid it right at Jessie's feet.

"Basically, we're out of money. When you can't even persuade Christians not to gamble, you're sunk. The donations have dried up. We're twelve thousand dollars in the hole. We'll probably have to close our doors, and then, mark my words, there'll be casinos and organized crime and harlots prowling our streets. You watch and see."

Lord, what have I done? I cared only for my own comfort. I sold out. Lord, forgive me, Jessie prayed.

There'd been no consoling her. It had been the worst month and a half of her life. She called the state lottery office to see if they'd take the money back, but they wouldn't. She wanted to buy a toaster, then give the rest of the money away. She talked about it with Asa at the supper table in late September.

"We need to be shed of that money. Every day it sits in our bank account is a charge against our souls," she warned.

"I thought I could use some of it to finish rebuilding the barn. I need to get that barn up. I've nowhere to put the tractor."

"That barn is becoming a monument to our sin. We've made a mistake. Let's not compound our error."

Asa groaned. "Aw, Jessie, can't we keep the money? It's been so nice having a little extra. And what about our kids? Sure, they're on their own and doing okay, but what if one of them got sick? What then?"

"We can do what we did before we had the money. We can trust God to care for our needs."

"Oh, Jessie, you know I trust the Lord. You know I do."

"Good, then getting rid of that money will be an easy matter."

But it hadn't been easy. They had put over three million dollars in certificates of deposit at Vernley's bank. Every month, Vernley sends them a check for twenty thousand dollars. Jessie and Asa have no idea what to do with it.

Jessie had sent ten thousand dollars to Brother Norman's shoe ministry to the Choctaw Indians, which infuriated the Friendly Women's Circle of Harmony Friends Meeting. The Circle had raised seven hundred dollars for Brother Norman at their annual Chicken Noodle Dinner during the Corn and Sausage Days festival. They were so proud. It was the most money they'd ever raised for the shoe ministry.

Jessie was the treasurer of the Circle. She'd sent Brother Norman a check from the Circle, and had enclosed her personal check for ten thousand dollars. Brother Norman had sent a thank-you card, which Frank the secretary had posted on the meetinghouse bulletin board.

Dear Jessie:
Thank you so much for your generous gift to our shoe ministry. You are truly a saint. I can't thank you enough.
Sincerely,
Brother Norman
P.S. Can you also thank the ladies for their donation?

"This is a fine state of affairs," Fern Hampton complained. "You work all year making noodles and you get a little P.S. thank you. But you can sell your soul and hit it rich, and people call you a saint. That's a fine how-do-you-do."

Every time Jessie and Asa gave money away, it made someone mad. They donated another ten thousand dollars to the town for a new playground for the children. They'd done it anonymously, but Bob Miles had figured it out and written about it in the *Herald. Anonymous Donors Give Money for Playground* read the headline, but he had put Jessie and Asa's twenty-fifth wedding anniversary picture underneath it.

Someone clipped out the article and put it in the hymnbook on Jessie and Asa's pew at church. They had written across the article,

Some people will do anything to get their picture in the paper. The next Sunday, Jessie opened the hymnal to number 127 to sing "Blessed Assurance" and the article floated to the floor at Dale Hinshaw's feet.

Dale reached down, picked it up, and handed it to Jessie, saying, "Proverbs 16:18." That was all he said. Proverbs 16:18.

During the quiet time, Jessie looked it up in her Bible. *Pride goeth before a fall,* she read.

She wanted to cry, sitting there in church, but she waited until she got home.

"And to think I gave Dale Hinshaw a chicken for his Scripture egg project," Asa fumed. "I've half a mind to take that chicken back."

He stewed about it for several days. Then on Tuesday he drove into town to Dale's house and knocked on his door.

"Hi, Asa. What brings you here?"

"I've come for my chicken."

"Uh, I thought it was mine to keep. Besides, it's one of my best layers."

"You should have thought of that before you insulted my wife."

"Boy, Fern Hampton was right when she said what she said."

"What did Fern say?"

140

"She said this money would go to your head and you'd forget who your friends were."

"I think we're finding out who our friends really are," Asa said, his voice rising. "And we've sure been surprised."

"I'll get your chicken."

Dale turned and clomped down the stairs to his basement. Asa could hear squawking, then Dale reappeared at the door with the chicken. He thrust it toward Asa.

"Here's your chicken. I'm just sorry it's come to this."

"No sorrier than I am."

"Does this mean you won't be making a donation toward the Scripture egg project?"

Asa didn't hear him. He was walking away, the chicken under his arm.

Asa didn't tell Jessie what had happened. She's the type who worries about hurting people's feelings. She worries about the woman from Fort Wayne who wrote the letter. She worries about the people from NAG and what they think of her. She's been brooding about the newspaper clipping in their hymnal.

"Never mind them," Asa tells her. "They're all busybodies. It's none of their business what we do."

Jessie dreaded the twenty-seventh day of the month, when the check came from the bank.

Clarence the mailman brought their September check on a Thursday. The window was bowed out from where he'd tried to see inside. He could just read the *Pay to the order of* part. Just enough to whet his interest.

"What do you think we ought to do with it?" Jessie asked Asa at the supper table.

"Well, I tell you one thing. We gave away the first check and it brought us nothing but heartache. I say we blow this one on ourselves."

They packed their suitcases the next afternoon and drove to the city to eat in a revolving restaurant atop a thirty-story building. They could see the water towers in the outlying towns, rising up like medieval towers. They took a room at a hotel that put chocolate mints on the pillows.

Asa poked around the bathroom. "Lookee here — shoeshine cloths. And they're free!"

"And there's a real safe in the closet," Jessie said. "With a combination and everything!"

They watched TV, then went to bed. They woke up the next morning and ordered breakfast in. A man brought it to their

142

room. It cost sixteen dollars. Asa gave him a twenty and told him to keep the change. They ate in bed, savoring the moment. It was the closest thing they'd ever had to a honeymoon. The only time they'd stayed in a hotel was the night before their daughter's wedding.

Asa smiled at Jessie. Jessie smiled back.

"Care for a strawberry?" he asked.

"Yes, thank you. Would you like some more tea?"

"Please." She poured him tea from a silver service.

Asa smiled at Jessie. Jessie smiled back.

"You look particularly lovely, Mrs. Peacock."

"And you're quite handsome."

Asa leaned back in bed and sighed. "You know, with all our money, we could maybe hire us a man to bring us breakfast in bed every Saturday."

Jessie laughed.

They finished their breakfast, then packed their bags, paid their bill, and drove west toward Harmony. Three miles from town they crested a hill and could see the town water tower in back of the school.

"Land ho," Asa cried out.

Jessie smiled. They rolled into town. Past Harvey Muldock's car dealership and the

Legal Grounds Coffee Shop. They stopped at the light next to Kivett's Five and Dime and waited for the light to turn.

"Honey, would you mind pulling over there in front of Kivett's?" Jessie asked, pointing to an empty space.

The light changed to green. Asa wrestled the truck into first gear and eased up in front of Kivett's.

"Why are we stopping here?" he asked.

"I'm going to buy a toaster. A four-slot toaster with a built-in bagel slicer, and I don't care what anyone thinks. I'm tired of caring what people think. We're going to do what we want and use the money however we wish, and if people don't like it, tough bananas."

She carried the toaster all the way home on her lap. She opened the box at the kitchen table and read the directions, then toasted four pieces of bread to a golden brown perfection.

She took her mother's silver service from the china cabinet in the living room and brewed a pot of tea. They sat at the table eating toast with strawberry jam, drinking their tea.

"Care for some more tea?" she asked Asa after a while.

"Please."

They ate in a companionable silence.

Jessie finished her toast and wiped her mouth. She sipped her tea. "You know, I've been thinking. Vernley's sending us twenty thousand dollars a month, but we can live on two thousand and that's with you quitting your job at the poultry plant. We break even with the farming. Why don't we give away the rest of it as the Lord leads us."

Asa smiled at her across the table. "You're a fine woman, Jessie Peacock."

"But first things first. How much money do we need to finish the barn?"

"Erven thinks it'll run another six thousand dollars, all told. That's with him and me doing the work."

"That leaves us twelve thousand dollars to give away this month. And I know just the folks to send it to."

She reached in her purse, pulled out their checkbook, and wrote a check for twelve thousand dollars to the Network Against Gambling.

"That ought to stir 'em up," Jessie said.

Asa laughed. "Jessie Peacock, you have a flair for the ironic."

She put the check in an envelope and addressed it to NAG, then fished a stamp from her purse.

Jessie and Asa walked down the lane to

the road, put the check in the mailbox, and raised the little metal flag. They ambled back up the lane, hand in hand. It was a beautiful early autumn afternoon, and all the world about them was verging on change.

Twelve

No More Wing Buds

The kids went back to school the Thursday after Labor Day. Harmony's townspeople woke to the sound of buses grinding up the hill near the park, and looked out their windows to see the children riding their bikes to school. The kids parked their bikes in the bike rack that Mr. Griswold, the janitor, had built under the tulip poplar behind the school.

Wayne Fleming got home from work just in time to drive his kids to school. It was a big day. Kate, his youngest, was entering kindergarten. Rachel was in first grade, and Adam in second.

Wayne drove them to school and walked them to their classes, then came back home, took a shower, and went to bed. The phone woke him up a little after lunchtime. It was the manager at the Kroger, asking if he could come in early that day to work.

Wayne had wanted to be home when his kids got out of school, but money has been a little tight so he agreed to go in. Adam needed braces, and Wayne's insurance didn't cover them. He called Deena Morrison to see if she could pick the kids up at school and bring them home.

"The neighbor lady can't be here until around seven," he explained. "I guess they can wait until then to eat supper."

"Nonsense. I'll take them to my house for supper. And I'll have them home by seven o'clock."

"I sure do thank you. They'll enjoy being with you."

"I'll enjoy being with them." She paused. "Are we still on for the Corn and Sausage Days parade this Saturday?"

Wayne had forgotten his promise to take Deena to the parade. What a mess, he thought.

"You bet we are, Deena. I'm looking forward to it. I just hope I feel up to it. I've been feeling a little puny lately."

"I'm sorry to hear that. I hope you get to feeling better. I miss seeing you."

"I miss seeing you, Deena."

They talked a little longer, then said good-bye.

A little before three, Deena hung the *Sorry, We're Closed* sign on the front door of the Legal Grounds Coffee Shop, climbed in her Jeep, and drove to the school to get the kids.

Adam, Rachel, and Kate came out of the school, saw Deena, and ran to her.

"What are you doing here?" Kate asked. "Where's Daddy?"

"Your daddy had to work, honey. But don't you worry. We're going to eat supper at my house."

She buckled them inside her Jeep and drove to her grandmother's house.

Mabel Morrison was sitting on her front porch when they turned in the driveway. She peered at the children. "Who have you brought home? Who are these children? I don't believe I've ever met them."

Kate laughed. "You know us. We're Deena's friends."

"Oh, so you are. Well, since we know one another, I suppose you can sit on my lap. Come on up here."

Kate climbed onto Mabel's lap. Adam sat on the porch rail, and Deena and Rachel sat on the porch swing. Rachel leaned into Deena.

"I have a secret," Kate whispered in Mabel's ear.

"Oh, I love secrets. Let me guess what it is." She squeezed her eyes shut and thought hard. "Does it have anything to do with an elephant?"

"No. You'll never guess, so I'll tell you.

My mommy's coming home."

Mabel Morrison's eyes opened wide. "Your mommy's coming home. Why, uh, that's nice, honey. I'll bet you're excited." She looked at Deena, who had turned rather pale.

Mabel turned back to Kate. "When's your mommy coming home?"

"This Saturday." She counted on her fingers. "In two days. Daddy said we'll all spend the day together, just like we used to." Kate turned to Deena. "Daddy said we could all go to the parade together. Do you want to come with us? You're our friend too."

Deena didn't hear her.

Kate tugged at her sleeve. "Will you go to the parade with us?"

Mabel lifted Kate from her lap and set her on the floor. "Kids, if you go into the kitchen, you'll find some cookies in the cookie jar. Adam, honey, can you be a big boy and pour the milk for your sisters?"

"Sure," he said. The kids opened the screen door and went inside.

"When did all this come about?" Mabel asked.

"It's the first I've heard of it. I wonder when Wayne was going to tell me . . ."

"Hopefully before Saturday." Mabel rose

150

from her rocker and sat beside Deena on the porch swing. She put her arm around her granddaughter. "I'm sorry, honey."

Deena's throat felt tight. Her eyes burned. "It's all right, Grandma. I'll be okay."

"Maybe when they're together this Saturday, he'll tell her he wants a divorce. Wouldn't that be wonderful?"

"Grandma, how can you say that? It would be sad. For their sake, I hope just the opposite happens. I hope they get the help they need, that they'll stay married, and that those precious children will have a mother again."

Mabel gave an indignant snort. "You can't be serious. What kind of mother would leave her children?"

"A mother who needs help. Now maybe she'll get it. In any event, I'll not stand between a man and his wife. I never should've dated Wayne in the first place."

The children returned to the porch, and Deena walked them to the park to play on the playground, then fed them supper before driving them home. The neighbor lady was waiting for them. Deena kissed the kids good-bye and gave them hugs. She'd always wanted children. Sometimes she imagined that Adam, Rachel, and Kate

151

were her children — that she and Wayne had married and they were all a family.

She hugged Katie to her, hard.

"Ouch," Kate said. "Be careful of my wing buds."

The week before, Kate had asked Deena what her shoulder blades were for, and Deena had told her they were wing buds — that when she became an angel, her wings would sprout from there.

Deena settled herself in the Jeep and drove home.

Her grandmother was standing at the stove, heating water for tea. There was a box of Kleenex on the table. Deena took one and scrunched it in her hand. Mabel poured her a cup of tea, then sat across from her.

"What am I going to do?" Deena moaned.

"Fight for your man."

"That's just it, Grandma. He's not my man. I was foolish to date him the first place. We're through. It's over."

"Don't be rash. You knew she'd be showing up sometime. Wait and see what happens."

"I just wish Wayne would've told me. I hate that I had to hear it from the kids."

"I'm sure he had a good reason for not

telling you yet. Why don't you ask him?"

"No. It's his place to tell me. I'm going to wait and see if he tells me."

She blew her nose and went upstairs to bed.

The next morning she woke and walked down to the Legal Grounds. As the coffee brewed, she watched out the window at the town kids making their way to school.

Wayne entered the shop a little after eight. He sat at the table near the window. Bea and Opal Majors were in the shop lingering over their coffee. Opal asked Deena for an apple muffin.

"Sorry," Deena said. "We're closing."

"Closing! What do you mean you're closing? Why are you closing?"

"Because the man just got here to spray for bugs. We're having a terrible cockroach problem."

Bea and Opal gathered their things and left.

Deena hung the *Sorry, We're Closed* sign on the front door and sat at the table across from Wayne.

"We need to talk," Wayne said.

"What about?"

This was the part Wayne hadn't been sure about — how to tell his girlfriend that his wife was coming home.

153

The week before, he'd gotten his hair cut and asked Kyle's advice.

"It doesn't really matter," Kyle told him. "You're sunk no matter how you do it."

Wayne groaned.

"Think about it," Kyle said. "Let's say you go back to Sally. There's no way Deena will have anything to do with you. And you'll be stuck with a woman who's left you once and will likely do it again. Every time she goes to the grocery store, you'll wonder if she's coming back. On the other hand, let's say Sally comes back here to live, but you marry Deena. There'll be a catfight for sure. Have you ever seen two women fight over a man?"

"Can't say as I have."

"I saw it in a movie once. It's nasty. All sorts of clawing and scratching and biting. And the worst part was that the man ended up getting blamed. No matter what you do, you're sunk. Do you want your neck shaved?"

"Sure."

"Have you considered becoming a priest and being celibate?"

"Not even for a moment."

"Then you better tell Deena, and the sooner the better. Just come right out and tell her."

So that's what Wayne did in the Legal Grounds Coffee Shop. He reached across the table and took Deena's hand.

"Sally's coming home tomorrow," he said.

Deena turned her head away. She knew if she looked at him, she'd cry.

"I'm sorry I'm just now telling you. I've known for some time. I just couldn't bring myself to tell you. Please forgive me."

"How long will she be here?"

"Just for the weekend. She wants to see the kids."

"And the kids want to see her, of course. I think it's nice they'll be together."

"I need to be there. I don't want to leave the kids alone with her just yet. I won't be able to take you to the parade."

"I understand." She pulled her hand from his. "Is she just coming to see the kids? Did she say anything about wanting to see you?"

"She said she hoped we could maybe work things out, but I don't want to. She had her chance."

"I see."

"Are you mad?"

"No, I'm not mad." Deena hesitated, then gathered up her courage. "But Wayne, I don't think we should date any longer. You need to be with your wife and get help for your marriage. You owe that to your children. And you can't do that if you're dating me."

"Oh, Deena, don't do this. My marriage is over. I'm telling Sally tomorrow. You're the one I want."

"I'll not do it this way. I'll not take a man from his wife. Not if she wants to try and make it work. I won't do it. Talk with her. Get counseling. Fix your marriage. You owe it to the kids." She rose from her chair. "Thank you for the past few months. I've enjoyed getting to know you and the kids. I wish you and Sally all the luck in the world. Now if you'll excuse me, I have work to do."

"Can we still go to church together? I won't try to hold your hand or anything."

"I don't think so. It wouldn't be right."

Deena went to the front door and turned the sign around to read *Yes, We're Open.* She walked behind the counter and poured out the old coffee.

Wayne stood and opened the door. The bell overhead tinkled. He walked out. The door swung closed behind him.

Deena stood at the sink, watching the coffee swirl down the drain, listening to the bell jingle fade away.

It's all gone. No more Wayne, no more kids, no more Sunday mornings at church, no more picnics. No more wing buds.

What surprised her most was the hurt. The aching hurt of failed love whimpering to a sad and lonely end.

Thirteen

A Sweet Liberation

It took Sam until October to work up the courage to tell the elders of his struggle to believe.

He had been primed to tell them at the September elders meeting. But when Miriam Hodge asked if there was any new business to discuss, they'd talked for three hours about whether they should get a building permit for the church's new gymnasium.

The elders were sharply divided. There was the "Let Every Person Be Subject to the Governing Authorities" faction, who believed that the Apostle Paul's injunction to the Christians in Rome supported the use of building permits. This group was led by Miriam Hodge. Then there was the "We Must Obey God Rather Than Man" faction, who believed that the Apostle Peter's defense before the high priests was an argument against building permits. They were headed up by Dale Hinshaw.

The elders argued for three hours before Miriam announced, "It's getting late and we're tired. We'll talk about this again next month. Is there any other new business?"

Sam didn't think it was the best time to tell them he didn't believe in God, so he kept quiet.

Now it was the third Thursday of October. Sam arrived at the meetinghouse early and sat on the steps waiting for Miriam to arrive. She pulled up to the curb in her truck.

"Hi, Miriam. How are you?" he asked, as she walked up the steps.

"Weary," she said, sitting beside him. "I'm not sure I'm up to another building-permit discussion."

"Maybe we can give them something else to talk about. I've got something to tell the elders, and I'd prefer to do it right up front."

Miriam looked at him. "Sam, is everything all right? You're not leaving us, are you? I know you've been pretty frustrated."

"No, I'm not leaving. At least not right now. I just need to talk with the elders."

The elders began pulling up to the meetinghouse in their cars. They tromped downstairs to the basement and sat at the folding table next to the noodle freezer. Miriam opened with a prayer, then said, "Before we begin our meeting, Sam has something he would like to say."

159

"Uh, thank you, Miriam. Well, I just thought you ought to know that I'm not sure I believe in God anymore."

When he said it out loud, it sounded more blunt than he'd intended. So he added, "It's not that I don't want to believe. I've been praying for God to be real to me. It's just that nothing's happened, and I've grown discouraged. I've got these doubts. And I just thought you should know . . . and that maybe you could help me."

Everyone stared at Sam.

Dale Hinshaw was the first to speak. "What do you mean you don't believe in God? You have to believe in God. It says so in the rules." He reached in his briefcase, pulled out a copy of *Quaker Faith and Practice*, and thumbed to the first page. "It says right here that we believe in one holy, almighty, all-wise, and everlasting God. I told you when you went away to that fancy seminary this would happen. Don't you remember? If you'd have just listened to me, it wouldn't have come to this."

"Oh, Lord," Fern Hampton wailed. "We have a minister who doesn't believe in God. No wonder this church is in such sorry shape."

Harvey Muldock said, "You know, Sam, when I'm going through a hard time, I buy

160

something. Why don't you stop past the dealership tomorrow and we'll see if we can't work you a deal on a new car. That ought to boost your spirits."

"Thanks, Harvey, but I don't think a new car will help."

"I think we should be tape-recording this meeting," Dale said. "Just in case we end up firing Sam. That way we'll be protected if there's a lawsuit."

"Oh, for goodness sakes. We're not going to fire Sam," Miriam scolded. "Get that idea out of your head."

"We can't let this get out," Fern wailed. "What will people think? They'll think we're all atheists, that's what they'll think. There go our chicken noodle sales. Did you think about that, Sam? Did you think how this might affect our noodle sales? Of course you didn't. You were too busy thinking about yourself. It used to be if people didn't believe in God they had the Christian decency to keep it to themselves."

Sam hung his head. This is what I get for casting my cares on the body of believers, he thought.

Asa Peacock cleared his throat. "I think we're being too hard on Sam. He's come to us with a problem, and I think we need to help him, just like he would help us if we were struggling. Sam, what can we do for you?" Asa reached across the table and laid his hand on Sam's.

Sam wanted to cry. He struggled to keep his voice even. "Thank you, Asa. I don't know what you can do. I just don't know. I've lost my faith. Lost my hope. I'm empty inside. Just plain empty. I've been praying, but nothing's changed."

"Well, of course nothing's changed," Dale said. "God doesn't answer the prayers of a man who doesn't believe in Him."

"Does this mean you have to believe in God before asking God to help you believe in Him?" Miriam asked.

"That's what it means," Dale said, a satisfied smile on his face. "That's how it works."

"Well, I've never heard of such foolishness," Asa said. "It seems to me God would welcome the prayers of a struggling man."

Dale started to say something, but Miriam saw where it was headed — before long they'd be embroiled in a three-hour theological debate on whether God listens to the prayers of a struggling man. She interrupted him. "Sam, I want to thank you for being honest about your doubts. I can't help but think we're partly to blame. I'm certain we've been a discouragement to you

162

in many ways." She paused, and her voice softened. "It has been my experience that doubts about God always begin with doubts about people. I know when you came here you had high hopes for our little church. I suspect we haven't always been enthusiastic. We could, and should, have done more."

"Well, you can't blame me," Dale said. "I've done my part. The Scripture egg project this year. Last year, I brought in Billy Bundle to preach the revival. And don't forget my signs."

"I'm sure we'll never forget your signs," Miriam assured him.

Dale had put up Burma Shave–style signs in front of Harvey Muldock's car dealership: *Go to church, and learn to pray. Or when you die, there's Hell to pay.* On the west edge of town he'd erected signs reading, *If you cheat, and drink and lie, turn to God, before you die.*

"It's not like *I've* been slacking off, either," Fern said. "Thanks to me, we have a new low-flow toilet in the women's bathroom, plus an oak-grained vanity. *I've* not been shirking my Christian duty."

"I'm not suggesting we've been lazy," Miriam said. "I just wonder if we've forgotten why we're here."

"I know why I'm here," Harvey Muldock said.

"Why is that?" Miriam asked.

"I'm here because my parents were members of this church and their parents before them. In fact, it was my great-great-great-grandfather, William Muldock, who helped start this church. That's why I'm here."

"But why did he start this church?"

"Well, near as I can tell, he got mad at the Quakers over at Sugar Grove and decided to start a new Quaker church here in town."

Miriam sighed. "Let me put it another way. What do you suppose God is calling us to do as His people?"

There was silence.

"Raise money for Brother Norman's shoe ministry to the Choctaw Indians," Fern ventured.

"I'm sure that's part of it. Any other ideas about what God is calling us to do?"

"Spread His Word through my Scripture egg project," Dale said.

"I'm certain God wants us to tell others about Him." Though I doubt your Scripture eggs are what He had in mind, Miriam thought to herself.

Sam was studying the plastic wood-grain swirl on the folding table. He raised his head. "I think God wants to love the world through Harmony Friends Meeting," he said.

"Bingo!" cried Miriam.

"Bingo? Now why didn't I think of that?" Fern said. "We could make a lot of money holding bingo games. The Catholics clean up. No reason we couldn't."

"Not that kind of bingo," Miriam said. "I was simply agreeing with Sam. He said he thought God wanted to love the world through Harmony Friends Meeting, and I was agreeing with him."

"Sounds like a lot of work. Wouldn't it be easier to hold a bingo game on Saturday nights and give the money to Brother Norman?"

"I don't think it would be right for the church to play bingo," Asa said. "Bingo is gambling, pure and simple."

"Look at the pot calling the kettle black, Mr. Lottery Millionaire himself," Fern huffed.

"We're not here to talk about bingo," Miriam said. "Bingo is not on the agenda. We're here to help Sam understand why he is discouraged. Though the longer we talk, the more it's becoming clear how it might have happened."

Asa said, "Sam, I asked earlier what we

165

could do to help you. Have you had any thoughts?"

Sam hesitated before speaking. "There is one thing. Preaching hasn't been easy. I can do everything else — visit the sick, fill out the paperwork, attend the meetings — but I feel like a hypocrite preaching. Standing up there telling you folks to believe something I don't believe myself. I just can't do it any-more."

"What would you propose we do?" asked Miriam.

Sam thought for several moments, then said, "Well, you're the elders of the meeting. Why don't you do the preaching?"

"We'll have to cut your pay," said Dale. "I'd like to recommend that we give Sam's pay to my Scripture egg project."

"We'll do no such thing," Asa said. "We pay him peanuts as it is."

"Sam, I think your idea is splendid," Miriam said. "We can do the preaching. We can take turns. Give you time to work through this. Do the rest of you approve?"

"If we don't want to preach, can we just find someone who can?" Harvey asked.

"Certainly." Then Miriam thought of Billy Bundle, the World's Shortest Evangelist. "But I'd like to suggest that whoever preaches needs to first be okayed by the elders."

The elders rumbled their approval.

Miriam said, "I can start. I'll preach this Sunday, then Dale, then Harvey, then Asa, then Fern."

"Can I preach about my Scripture egg project?" Dale asked.

"Dale, you preach on whatever the Lord lays on your heart. Now as the elders of this meeting, we're going to pray for Sam. I want you to stand up and gather around him."

"Can't we pray sitting down?" Fern asked.

"No, we're going to put our hands on Sam's head and pray for him."

Asa walked around the table and stood behind Sam, laying his hand on Sam's head. Then followed Dale and Harvey and Miriam, and finally Fern, with a heavy, inconvenienced sigh.

"Lord," Miriam prayed, "we pray for your servant Sam. We ask your forgiveness for failing you and failing Sam. We've not been the church you called us to be. We repent of our apathy and self-centeredness. Forgive us. Restore Sam. Strengthen his faith and deepen his love for you, Lord. Amen."

The elders stood around Sam, silent, their hands on his head.

A tear slid down Sam's cheek. "Lord,

ignite my heart," he prayed in a whisper.

"And while you're at it, Lord, bless my Scripture egg project," Dale said.

"Lord, tell us what to preach," Asa prayed. "Help us help your church. Amen."

"Amen," rumbled the elders.

There was more silence. Fern raised her hand from Sam's head, then Miriam and Harvey and Dale, and finally Asa.

"We love you, Sam," Miriam said. "Don't you forget that. And even though you don't believe in God just now, He believes in you. You'll remember that, won't you?"

She hugged him to her.

"I'll remember."

Asa and Dale and Harvey shook his hand. Fern smiled at him, though not too big a smile.

"I just hope this doesn't affect our noodle sales," she said.

They turned off the lights in the basement and walked up the stairs out into the autumn evening. The elders climbed into their cars and drove away, while Sam walked the four blocks down Main Street to Washington Street to his home.

He felt light. His step was buoyant. Honesty is a sweet liberation, he thought.

He walked up the stairs, across the porch, and through the door. Barbara and the boys were in their beds. He kissed the boys good night, then brushed his teeth, and lay down beside his wife.

He wrapped his arm around her and pulled her to him.

A sweet liberation, he thought as he drifted off to sleep.

Fourteen

On the Night of Love Reborn

Sally Fleming had been at the trailer going on five weeks. She came into town with all her clothes the Saturday afternoon of the Corn and Sausage Days parade, and she hadn't left. Wayne thought Sally had come only for the weekend, but on Monday morning she didn't leave and she's been there ever since. He's not sure how it happened, but Sally ended up with the bed and he's been sleeping on the pull-out sofa with a bar in his back.

Wayne wanted to ask his wife where she'd been for the past year, but he hates conflict. He's been hoping Sally will volunteer the information, but so far she's kept quiet.

Wayne talked with Kyle Weathers about it during a haircut.

"Do you suppose I oughta ask her where she's been?" he asked.

Kyle spun the barber's chair around, stared at Wayne, then tapped Wayne's head with his knuckles. "Hello in there. Is anyone home? Your wife was gone for more than a year, she's been home for five weeks, and you still haven't talked about it?!

What's wrong with you?"

"Yeah, well, I guess I didn't want to upset her."

Kyle shook his head. "Wayne Fleming, you are a doormat."

It doesn't look like Sally Fleming will be leaving anytime soon. She read in the *Herald* classifieds of a job opening for a receptionist at the mental-health center. She drove into town to apply and was hired, which upset certain people to no end. It was a good job and paid well, contradicting everything certain people had been taught about God's sure justice.

"I guess the wages of sin aren't death after all," Bea Majors said to Fern Hampton.

"What is this world coming to when someone will hire a known adulteress?" Fern harrumphed.

"I've said all along that this mental-health stuff was invented so the liberals could feel good about their sin," Dale Hinshaw said.

But what really got certain people stirred up was when Sally came to church with Wayne and their kids and sat in the Wilbur Matthews pew.

"Did you see that little chippy just march into the church like she owned the place?" Fern said to Bea afterward. "I'm glad my mother's not alive to see this desecration.

And did you see Sam? He shook her hand and invited her back! Used to be ministers of the gospel knew how to deal with sinners — and it wasn't with a handshake, let me tell you. It was with a Bible upside the head!"

Fern's term as an elder expires in December, but she's thinking of nominating herself for another three years and becoming head elder so she can muscle things through. She wants to see the new gymnasium built, with her mother's name on a plaque above the door. But before she does that, she wants to put Sally Fleming in her right and proper place, which is down the road at the Harmony Worship Center, where they wink at sin, so long as you tithe.

Wayne isn't sure what to think of Sally being home. He's glad for his children, but he's confused. It's one thing to be a forgiving Christian and remember sin no more, but some things are easier said than done.

Then Sally asked Wayne to come back to their bed, but so far he's kept to the couch. It's his line in the sand. "Not until we've talked to Sam and gotten counseling," he told her.

"Isn't it enough that I'm sorry?"

"No, it isn't."

On Sally's first Sunday at church, Dale Hinshaw preached on the seventh commandment: "Thou Shalt Not Commit Adultery." Fern Hampton turned and glared at Sally as Dale preached. Sally lowered her head and watched her knees the entire sermon. Wayne wishes someone would preach a sermon about self-righteousness so he could glare at Fern.

He sits in church on Sunday mornings with Sally and the kids, but he thinks of Deena and what might have been.

Deena has moved up to the fourth row, to the Hodge pew, next to Amanda Hodge. Wayne watches her from three rows back. Sometimes she turns her head and he can see her face, and the pain of his loss is scarcely bearable.

He hasn't talked with Deena since Sally came home. He stopped by the Legal Grounds one Saturday morning in early November, but Deena had stepped out to go to the bank. Mabel waited on Wayne.

"How's Deena doing?" he asked her.

"Her heart's broke, but other than that, she's fine."

"I guess that's my fault."

"It's no one's fault. It's just life. It's the risk of caring for someone." Mabel sat down next to him. "How are you, Wayne? You don't look well."

"I don't feel well. I don't know what to do."

"Lot of that going around. How are things going with you and Sally?"

"Who knows? She won't talk about it. She won't get counseling. She seems to think everything can be the way it was before she left."

"Well, I imagine she feels awfully bad about what she did and just wants to put it behind her."

"I don't like dwelling on it myself, but I do think we have some talking to do, and she won't," Wayne said.

"It's none of my business, but I think Sally owes you an explanation and owes it to you and the kids to get some counseling."

"I agree. We'll see what happens." He rose and put two dollars on the table. "There's for the coffee. Can you tell Deena hi for me?"

"Sure, I'll tell her, Wayne." Mabel stood and gave Wayne a hug. "I'm sorry it didn't work out for you and Deena." She paused. "I probably shouldn't tell you this, but Deena's got a job offer from a law firm in the city, and she's thinking pretty strong about taking it."

Wayne drove home to the trailer. The kids were playing outside. Sally was sitting on the steps, bundled in a jacket, watching. He sat down beside her.

"I'm only going to say this once, Sally, so listen close. I'm calling Sam to set up a time we can talk with him. If you don't go with me, we're through."

Sally began to cry.

"We need help, Sally. Will you talk to him or not?"

The kids had stopped playing and were watching. Katie began to cry.

"You're upsetting Katie," Sally said.

"And your running off for over a year didn't trouble her at all?"

"I had my reasons."

"What were they? You owe us that much. Why'd you leave us? Tell us now or we're through, Sal. So help me God, I'll throw you out." He was shaking with anger.

Sally sobbed.

He stood to his feet. "Come on, kids, we're leaving for a while." He reached in his wallet and pulled out forty dollars. He placed the money on the step next to Sally. "You take this. I'm going with the kids into town to the playground. I'll be back in one hour. I want you gone when I get home."

175

Sally shook with the crying. "You don't understand."

"I understand that you cheated on me."

"I never did. I never once did."

"You expect me to believe that? Everyone knows about it. That's why they look at you the way they do."

"I never once cheated on you."

"Then why'd you go away? Why'd you leave us? Tell me."

Sally wiped her sleeve across her face, then spoke in a whisper. "I'm sick. Bad sick."

"Sick? What do you mean you're sick? What are you talking about?"

"Remember last year when we thought I was pregnant and I went to the doctor to be tested? Well, I wasn't pregnant."

"I know. You told me so yourself."

"But what I didn't tell you was that one of the blood tests came back wrong."

Wayne sat down on the step. "What do you mean one of the tests came back wrong?"

"It was my white blood cells. The count was way up. They ran a few more tests, and I've got something bad wrong with me. It's some kind of leukemia."

He felt the breath go out of him. "Oh, Sally, why didn't you tell me?"

"I didn't tell you because I didn't want to put you and the kids through all that. That's why I let it out that I was gonna run off with someone. I figured if you was mad at me, it'd be easier to get on with your life."

Wayne reached over and pulled Sally to him. It was the first time in over a year he had really touched her. She felt small and fragile in his arms, like a caught bird. "My Lord, Sally, why in the world didn't you tell me? I could've helped you." He pulled her closer so her head tucked under his chin. "I could've helped you."

"I was scared. Scared of worrying the kids. Scared of being a burden. Scared of dying. Scared you'd stop loving me."

"I'd never have stopped loving you. You should've told me. We'd have made it."

"I can't tell you how hard the past year has been for me. I've missed you and the kids so much. Cried myself to sleep every night thinking of you. Worried myself sick wondering how you and the kids were getting along." She began to cry again.

"We're together now," he said. "That's all that matters. You watch, this will all work out."

Katie was staring at them. "What's wrong, Daddy?" she asked in a small, wounded voice. "Why's Mommy crying?"

He pulled little Katie to him with his other arm. His mind was racing. This is too much. Lord, why are you letting this happen?

"Mommy's sick," Wayne said, as calmly as he could. "But don't you worry. The doctors are going to make her well. Don't you worry."

"Is that right, Mommy?" Katie asked. "Are the doctors going to make you all better?"

"They sure will, honey." Sally wiped her eyes and stood up. "Let's get cleaned up from playing and I'll make you some lunch."

After lunch, Wayne, Sally, and the kids piled into the truck and drove to the park in town. Then they went grocery shopping and for a drive through the country. They ended up in Cartersburg at the Dog 'n' Suds for supper, the kids sandwiched in the truck between Wayne and Sally, eating their hot dogs.

Winter was coming. It was a little after six, and the sun was dropping. The wind had a chill to it. Wayne reached over and turned the heater on. The smell of burnt dust filled the cab.

He started the truck, backed out, and drove down the highway toward home.

They gave the kids a bath, then Sally read them a story and put them to bed.

She came into the living room and lay on the couch with her head in Wayne's lap. He stroked her hair.

"What are we going to do?" he asked.

"I talked with Doctor Neely last week. He's going to refer me to a doctor in the city for some testing."

Wayne felt like crying. "How much longer . . . uh . . ." He couldn't bring himself to finish the question.

"He wouldn't say. He said it's the slow type of leukemia, and that they know a lot more about it than they used to. Can we not talk about it right now? I just want you to hold me."

Wayne held her to him. "Would you mind if I move back into our bedroom?" he asked in a quiet voice.

"I was hoping you would."

"We don't have to . . . you know . . . I can just hold you, if that's all you want. I'd be just as happy holding you."

Sally smiled. It was the first thing he'd loved about her. Her smile.

"We can start with holding, but I think we should be open to further possibilities."

"Well, Mrs. Fleming, if that's your recommendation, I will honor it."

★ ★ ★

Outside the trailer, winter was coming on. A skiff of snow blew across the fields. A car drove past on the highway. The driver looked at the sagging, tired trailer, saw the lights go off, and felt the cold push of a northern wind nudge his car toward the shoulder.

"Wouldn't you hate living there?" the driver said to his wife.

"I can't imagine anything worse."

But back in the trailer, on that night of love reborn, there was no other place Wayne and Sally would rather have been than in their little trailer, with all the world at bay.

Fifteen

A Beautiful Week

It was the week of Thanksgiving, and it had been beautiful. A strong north wind blew through on Monday, bringing down the last of the leaves. The rest of the week was crisp and sunny. People put on their flannel shirts and blue jeans and took to their yards to rake the leaves out to the gutter and burn them.

Harvey Muldock left work on Saturday afternoon and went for a walk through town. Autumn is Harvey's favorite season. He likes the smell of it, the pungency. Especially the burning.

Bob Miles had written an editorial in the *Herald* opposing leaf burning and cautioning against global warming. Harvey was going to write an anonymous rebuttal exposing the myth of global warming, but it had been such a beautiful week he let it pass — the kind of week where you don't want to argue with anyone for fear it will blemish the perfection.

Besides, Harvey's mind was fixed elsewhere. It was his week to bring the message at Harmony Friends Meeting, and he'd been pondering what to preach. He was thinking of talking about how autumn is the season of dying, but that spring brings new life and thus is God's encouragement for us to remain faithful in the face of death. A depressing topic for such a beautiful week, but something worth bearing in mind.

The Sunday before Thanksgiving, Asa Peacock had preached on being grateful. Asa is a grateful man these days. He and Jessie have been enjoying their lottery money. They get their check on the twenty-seventh of the month, lay it on the kitchen table, and pray over it, asking the Lord to lead them in its use. They've given money to feed children in Africa, donated fifteen thousand dollars to a Romanian orphanage, and paid for Opal Majors to have her hammertoe corrected.

That Tuesday, Asa went to visit Dale Hinshaw to apologize for taking back his chicken. He returned the chicken to Dale, and it felt so good not having anything against anyone. He felt so noble.

He and Jessie got another check the day after Thanksgiving. They're not sure how to spend it, but they're praying about it.

"Lord, show us who to help," they pray. "Open our eyes."

They've been giving Sam Gardner a thousand dollars a month. They thought money worries might be one reason for Sam's discouragement. He doesn't earn much money being a Quaker pastor, and every time he brings up the subject of a raise Fern Hampton says, "I thought Quaker pastors were supposed to live simply."

Fern is an advocate of simplicity so long as it doesn't involve her.

With the children in school, Sam's wife had interviewed for the receptionist's job at the mental-health center, but was told she had too much education. They gave the job to Sally Fleming instead.

Sam hadn't realized how resentful he'd grown over the years. Even with all his college, he'd never earned more than thirty thousand dollars a year. He didn't mind the low salary when he was starting in the pastorate, but he's grown tired of telling his boys "We can't afford it" every time they ask for something.

"Just once," he'd said to Barbara, "I'd like to buy them new bicycles. Just to see the look on their faces."

Then one Sunday in October, as Sam was shaking hands at the door after church, Jessie slipped him an envelope with a thousand dollars in it. There was a note in the envelope telling Sam how much they appreciated his ministry and that they'd be giving him a thousand dollars a month. He couldn't believe it. In a moment of prideful dignity he was going to turn it down, but then he changed his mind. Instead, he bought his boys new bicycles, bought Barbara a new dress she'd been admiring, and paid down their bills.

What Sam appreciated most was the quiet manner in which the Peacocks gave him the money. The Christmas before, the church had given Sam a check for twenty-five dollars. They'd handed him the money during church, in front of everyone, expecting him to gush over it.

"The tightwads," he'd complained to his wife that night. "I work sixty hours a week. I'm on call twenty-four hours a day, seven days a week. I didn't get all my vacation this year. And they expect me to slobber with gratitude when they hand me twenty-five bucks?"

It's one thing to spend your life in a noble cause, but another matter entirely to be taken for granted.

Sam has been sitting in the fifth row with his family while the elders have been preaching. It feels odd sitting there. People watch him to see if he closes his eyes during the prayers. Everyone in the church knows of his struggle. Fern Hampton let it slip in the October meeting of the Friendly Women's Circle. She hadn't intended to tell, but it was such a marvelous secret — *a pastor's loss of faith!* — she couldn't help herself. She told Bea Majors, who wrote about it in the church column in the *Harmony Herald*:

The elders at Harmony Friends Meeting will be preaching until Sam Gardner believes in God again.

All over town, folks have been talking about it. The old men down at the Coffee Cup ruminate about it over their bacon and eggs. An atheist pastor. Some of them are thinking of going to church just to see what happens.

Some people are no longer speaking to Sam, which has been the only blessing of this whole ordeal. Dale Hinshaw has quit asking his help on the Scripture egg project.

"Nothing personal, Sam," he told him. "I just can't afford to anger the Lord by letting a pagan help me. I can't risk the taint."

They prayed for Sam at the November meeting of the Harmony Ministerial Association. It was their meeting to nominate new officers. The month before, they had asked

185

Sam to be the new president, but after reading the *Herald* they retracted their nomination.

When they'd first asked Sam to serve, he'd been reluctant. "I'm busy enough as it is," he'd told them. "I don't think I have the time for such an important job."

"Oh, it's not that important" they'd said. "You pretty much just run the meetings, that's all."

But when they learned of Sam's struggle, they told him, "The president of the association is a symbol of our community's faith. We need to find someone the town can look up to. Besides, some of the churches are going to cut their donations if you're the president. We'd hate for it to come down to a vote, so if you could just withdraw your name, we'd be grateful."

So he did.

The pastor of the Harmony Worship Center wanted to kick Sam out of the association altogether.

"Nothing personal," he'd told Sam. "But it sends the wrong message to our children to have an unbeliever in the association."

Sam was tired of hearing he shouldn't take things personally. "I've been called a pagan and a threat to children, but I'm not supposed to take it personally?" he com-

186

plained to Barbara.

"I told him to keep quiet about it," she told her mother on the phone the Tuesday before Thanksgiving. "But, no, he thinks he has to be a man of integrity and tell everyone what he's thinking. For crying out loud, they even put it in the paper."

That's what had really set her off. She had marched down to the *Herald* office the day the paper came out.

Bob Miles was sitting behind his desk by the front window. He could see her marching down the sidewalk, clutching the paper. There wasn't time to hide.

She flung the door open and stepped into his office.

"I'm sorry," he said, before she'd even spoken. "I missed it. Bea sent it over, and Arvella typed it in. I never saw it or I'd have left it out. I'll run a retraction if you want."

Barbara didn't say anything. She just stood there shaking, then stormed out of the office, muttering under her breath about pastors' families living under a microscope.

Other than that, it had been a beautiful week.

Asa and Jessie Peacock's daughter, Susan, flew in Wednesday for Thanksgiving. Asa met her at the airport in the city.

She lives in Colorado and is married to a lawyer. They decided early in their marriage not to have children. They have a cat instead.

Susan and her mother were doing dishes after the Thanksgiving dinner.

"Any chance of me becoming a grandmother?" Jessie pried.

"I don't think so, Mom. Mark and I enjoy being child-free."

That night Jessie complained to Asa, "You'd think children were a disease, the way she talks about them. Child-free! What kind of talk is that?"

"Maybe they don't think they can afford children."

"If that's all it is, let's give them money."

Asa thought about that for a moment. "That doesn't seem right to me. Paying our daughter to have children."

Jessie sighed. "No, I guess not."

Their son, David, and his wife want to have children but can't. It has something to do with David.

"Have you tried wearing boxer shorts?" Jessie asked him one day. "I heard on *Oprah* that boxer shorts can, uh, help things in that area."

She's thinking of buying him boxer shorts for Christmas.

Jessie goes to the Friendly Women's Circle on Tuesday mornings to roll out noodles. When the ladies take a coffee break and pull out pictures of their grandchildren, Jessie just sits quietly, sipping her coffee.

"You need to get your kids going on some children," Fern Hampton says.

Jessie just smiles.

Their daughter stayed until Saturday, then Jessie and Asa drove her to the airport so she could fly home to Colorado. They stopped for lunch at a Big Boy Restaurant along the interstate just outside the city, then came on home.

They passed Harvey Muldock as he strolled through town. Asa eased to the curb and rolled down his window.

"Hi, Harvey."

"Hey there, Asa. Hi, Jessie. What brings you all into town?"

"We're coming back from taking Susan to the airport," Asa said. "What're you doing?"

"I'm thinking about my sermon. Tomorrow's my turn to preach."

"Oh, that's right. Well, it's not so bad. You'll come up with something. Just remember to keep it short."

Harvey laughed. "You got that right."

Asa put the truck in gear. "Good luck tomorrow, Harvey. We'll be thinking of you."

"Appreciate that, Asa. I really do."

Asa pulled away from the curb. Harvey stood on the sidewalk, inhaling the scent of burning leaves and thinking.

When Miriam Hodge had volunteered the elders to preach, he'd been opposed to it. "That's what we pay Sam to do," Harvey had complained to his wife. "Why can't he just fake it?"

But now he doesn't think it's such a bad idea. He especially liked Miriam's message a couple weeks before. She talked about the sympathy of God, how all through the Bible people struggled to believe and how gracious God was to deepen their faith. Harvey was glad to hear that. He's getting older. Sometimes he thinks about dying and wonders whether everything he's been taught about heaven is true.

It's a comfort to believe God might not mind his doubts.

In her sermon, Miriam had said that doubt can be the beginning of belief. Harvey's been thinking about that and believes she might be right. Doubts lead to questions, which, if we're patient enough, eventually lead to answers. Harvey thought about preaching on the benefits of doubting but didn't want to upset Dale Hinshaw, who's still not speaking to Miriam after her sermon. So he'll probably preach about how autumn is the season of dying, but that spring brings new life and thus is God's encouragement for us to remain faithful in the face of death.

Sixteen

Peace on Earth

It was a Tuesday morning in early December, and Bob Miles was watching the town square from his desk by the window of the *Harmony Herald*.

It was a big day for Bob — he was writing the one-thousandth edition of "The Bobservation Post." He hadn't told anyone, though he was hoping to work it into conversation. He'd spent a lot of time at the Coffee Cup the day before, waiting for someone to say, "Hey, Bob, how long you been writing that column anyway?"

Then he could've answered, in an off-handed kind of way, "Well, I'm not certain, but I think this week is my thousandth one." Maybe Penny Toricelli would overhear him and bake a cake, and they'd have a little party in honor of "The Bobservation Post."

But it didn't happen. Instead, he sat on a stool at the Coffee Cup as Penny swiped the counter in front of him and said, "Say, Bob, there was a misprint in last week's ad. Italian Night is Wednesday night, not Thursday night."

Italian Night was Vinny Toricelli's idea. He'd read in a magazine that ethnic restaurants were all the rage, so he'd bought a used organ at an auction and put it in the corner next to the salad bar underneath the painting of the Last Supper. He hired Bea Majors to play the organ from five to seven o'clock every Wednesday night. Vinny wanted her to play until eight o'clock, but Bea doesn't want to miss *Jeopardy!*, so she leaves five minutes before seven and gets home just in time to watch Alex Trebeck, who, she is certain, appreciates her viewing loyalty.

Bob was sitting at his desk on Tuesday morning when he noticed Ned Kivett arranging a Christmas display in the front window of Kivett's Five and Dime. Ned's had the same display since 1956. Santa's suit is faded to pink, and the red paint on Rudolph's nose is mostly chipped off. Now Rudolph's nose just looks swollen, like he's been in a fight or had one too many drinks.

Why bother? Ned thinks. I'm the only store in town. So what if my decorations are cheesy? Where else can people shop?

For one hundred and seventy-five years this town has cultivated the fine art of indifference. Bob Miles gets an advertisement wrong and shrugs it off. Kyle Weathers leaves one sideburn longer than another and couldn't care less. But when Deena Morrison opened the Legal Grounds Coffee Shop it jarred the town's complacency. Penny and Vinny at the Coffee Cup had to snap to. It used to be if Penny spilled a little coffee, she'd snarl at you for jostling her arm and make you wipe up the mess. Now she smiles and says, "Don't you worry, honey. I'll take care of that." Vinny even took down their *Eat, Drink, and Be Quiet* sign and replaced it with one that reads *Through These Doors Pass the Finest People on Earth.*

All this politeness has made people edgy. If they had wanted polite, they'd have gone to the pastor's house for coffee. So they were relieved to hear that Deena might be closing down the Legal Grounds and moving back to the city to practice law. Life at the Coffee Cup could return to its former mediocrity, and everyone could relax.

But Deena hasn't moved yet. She visited her parents for Thanksgiving and stayed away an extra week. She hung a *Closed Until Further Notice* sign on the front door of the Legal Grounds. Everyone thought she'd left for good, but now she's back.

Bob Miles saw her coming around the corner in front of the Royal Theater, and his heart gave a little leap. He watched her unlock the Legal Grounds Coffee Shop door.

What a beautiful woman, he thought. That Wayne Fleming is an idiot.

That is the consensus of most everyone in town. They can't believe Wayne's taken his wife back after the way she'd run off the year before.

Bob Miles sees Sally Fleming nearly every morning. She walks past his window on the way to her new job at the mental-health center upstairs from the *Herald*. Sally is not without her charms. Blond hair and blue eyes and a warm smile. But the best thing about her is that she doesn't act like she's pretty. She smiles at everyone — even those who treat her like dirt, like Fern Hampton.

Back in November Fern had announced in church that they needed a volunteer for the primary Sunday school class. When Sally raised her hand, Fern looked right over her like she wasn't there. Everyone noticed it and looked down at their feet and studied the red carpet.

"That Fern Hampton has no business being in the church," Wayne fumed that night after the kids were in bed.

"Oh, never mind her," Sally said. "That's just the way she is. I kind of feel sorry for her. She must be miserable inside."

They had planned to tell the church about Sally's leukemia during the prayer time, but after Fern's slight they'd been so embarrassed they hadn't said anything.

Sam was the only one in church who knew. Wayne and Sally had made him promise not to tell anyone. They wouldn't even have told Sam, except they needed him and Barbara to watch their kids while they went to the cancer doctor in the city. But after they told him, it felt good to have someone else share the burden.

Sam had been stopping past once a week ever since. Then he'd invited them to his parents' house for Thanksgiving dinner. Sally brought dessert — Jell-O with little marshmallows — then helped wash dishes afterward while the men watched football and Barbara took the kids outside to play.

Sally washed while Sam's mother, Gloria Gardner, dried and put away. When Sally had been younger, she'd dreamed of moments like this. Her mother had died when she was five. She'd been raised by her father, who loved her but was too consumed with grief to pay her any mind. Sally would watch television shows of normal families, with mothers and everything. When her father did remarry, it was to a shrewish woman who didn't like Sally and let her know it. Which is why Sally married Wayne when she turned eighteen.

This is what it would have been like if Mom had lived, Sally said to herself. We would have spent Thanksgiving together, doing dishes and talking and laughing.

When she'd first learned of her leukemia, she had been mad at God. How could you do this to me? First you take my mother, now you'll leave my children without a mother. What kind of God are you?

Then one morning while the kids were in school, the thought struck her: I should go away before my children get to know me any better. It'll be easier on them that way. Looking back, she knows it was a dumb idea, and she's glad to be home.

She watched her children out the window, with Gloria standing beside her. The sorrow of it hit all at once. She ached for them. A tear slid down her cheek. Sam's mother looked over at her. She thought she'd pretend she didn't notice, but then Sally sobbed.

"Oh, there now, honey. What's wrong?" Gloria asked. She laid down her dishcloth, put her arm around Sally, and eased her over to the kitchen table.

Sally kept crying. Her shoulders trembled.

"My poor babies," she moaned.

"What's wrong, honey? You can tell me."

"I'm sick."

"Well, honey, let's get you home and into bed. You'll probably wake up tomorrow and be just fine."

"No, no, I won't. It's worse than that."

After some prodding, Sally told Gloria about the leukemia and how she was going to the cancer doctor to have tests run. By the time she was through, Wayne had come in the kitchen and was kneeling beside her, holding her. Sam and Charlie Gardner were watching from the kitchen door.

"I'm sorry," Sally sniffed. "I didn't mean to ruin everyone's Thanksgiving."

Gloria stared at her, ashen-faced. Leukemia . . . My Lord . . .

"Wayne, I think it's time to go home," Sally said, standing up from the chair and wiping her eyes with the heels of her hands. "Thank you, Mr. and Mrs. Gardner. It was kind of you to invite us. We're certainly grateful to you."

Gloria hugged Sally's thin body to her. "There now, it was our pleasure. You and your family are welcome anytime. We'd love to have you for Christmas. That is, if you don't have plans."

"We'd like that," Sally said.

"Now you just let us know if we can do

anything at all for you. Just anything at all. We'll be happy to help. Isn't that right, Charlie?"

"You bet."

After the Flemings left, the Gardners sat around the kitchen table talking.

"Did you know about this, Sam?" Gloria asked.

"Yeah, for a little over a month now."

"And why didn't you tell me?"

"Gee, Mom, I can't tell you everything. There are some things people tell me that I can't talk about. But I can tell you one thing . . ."

"What's that?"

"The leukemia is the reason she ran off. She didn't want the kids to see her sick and dying. Her mother died when she was little, and she didn't want to put them through that. She only came back because she missed them."

They sat around the table, quiet and thinking.

"Well, now that we know, I think we ought to do something," Gloria said.

"Like what?" Sam asked.

"I don't know. Maybe the Friendly Women's Circle could hold a bake sale for her. Lord knows, they'll need the money."

"That's a wonderful idea," Barbara said.

Sam's mother peered at the calendar on the refrigerator. "The Circle meets next week. I'll tell 'em then, when they're all together, and we can start the planning."

The Circle met the next Tuesday morning down in the church basement, at the folding table by the noodle freezer.

Gloria Gardner is the president, having maneuvered Fern Hampton out of the job the year before. Fern had been complaining how busy she was, so Gloria said, "We ask too much of you, Fern, that's all there is to it. Tell you what, I'll take over as president and give you a break."

Miriam Hodge had quickly seconded the motion, the other women said "Approved," and Fern was out, Gloria was in, and Fern's been mad ever since.

Gloria began the meeting with a tap of the sacred meat-tenderizing mallet on the folding table. The ladies stopped their talking and turned to look at her.

"We've got a problem," Gloria said. "It's Sally Fleming."

"What about that little chippy?" Fern asked. "Has she run off again?"

"She has leukemia," Gloria said.

There were gasps, then a collective "Oh, my" rose up from around the table.

They turned toward Gloria, enthralled. It was all they could do not to rush home to call people and tell them the news, to experience the exquisite joy of informing the uninformed.

Except for Miriam Hodge and Jessie Peacock, who bowed their heads and began to pray quietly for Sally.

"Well, I guess it's true that you reap what you sow," Fern said.

"What do you mean by that, Fern?" Gloria asked.

"I mean a person can't run off and sleep around without paying for it in the end."

"How do you know she slept around? Did she tell you?"

"Well, now, I'm not dumb. Everyone knows what she did. It's all over town."

Several of the women nodded in agreement.

"I think you ought to know something, Fern. Sally Fleming didn't run off with another man. She left her family because she didn't want her kids to watch her die. She only came back because she missed them. Although going away might not have been a wise thing to do, she did it for her kids."

Fern looked down at her lap, then inspected her fingernails. "Oh, I see," she said, in a quiet voice.

The ladies looked away from Fern. There was a long silence.

Fern opened her mouth to speak a time or two, but nothing came out. "I've been a hateful snot," she said, finally.

Though Fern Hampton has few virtues, it is true that occasionally she acts like the Christian she claims to be.

She stood from the folding table and excused herself. She lumbered up the stairs, her knees cracking, and went outside to her car. She drove down to the mental-health office, walked up the stairs, her knees cracking, and pushed open the door.

Sally was seated behind the desk. "Hi, Mrs. Hampton," she said with a smile.

"Hi, Sally," Fern said, and offered a timid smile herself.

"How can I help you? Did you want to talk with the therapist?"

"Oh my, no, nothing like that. I'm perfectly fine in that department. No, actually I wanted to talk with you, Sally." Fern paused. "Uh . . . well . . . I just want to tell you I'm sorry. I've treated you shamefully, and I ask your forgiveness."

She knows, Sally thought. "That's okay, Fern. I know you didn't mean anything by it."

"We'd be happy to have you teach that Sunday school class. That is, if you're able and still want to."

"I'd love nothing more. But I'll be starting my treatment before long. Can we wait and see how that goes?"

"Oh, yes, honey. You just work on getting better. Is there anything I can do for you?"

"Not that I can think of. But if something comes to mind, I'll be sure to let you know."

Fern reached down and drew Sally into her considerable bosom. "We'll be praying for you. Remember, if I can do anything at all, just let me know."

"I'll remember."

Bob Miles watched Fern Hampton pass in front of his window.

He was typing out the thousandth column of "The Bobservation Post." He wrote:

I see Fern Hampton leaving the mental-health center. Down the street, Ned Kivett is putting up his Christmas display. Can you believe another Christmas is upon us? Here's hoping for peace on earth and goodwill toward men.

He rolled the paper out of the typewriter and carried it over to the Linotype machine.

The one-thousandth column, he marveled. Who would ever have believed it!

Seventeen

A Winter Blessing

The first big snow of the season slipped into town on Saturday morning, three days before Christmas. People stayed up late to watch the news on Friday, then went to bed and awoke to find eight inches of snow piled on the ground.

Children all over town rummaged through garages looking for their sleds, then headed over to the park to the sledding hill above the basketball court. Charlie Gardner dug Sam's old Radio Flyer out from behind the lawn mower. He sanded the rust from the runners with steel wool, then waxed them slick with a stubby candle. He pulled the sled over to Sam's house, and he and Sam took Levi and Addison to the park.

Sam had intended to go to the office, but he decided to take the day off instead. He's been doing that quite a bit lately, and the world hasn't ended. He's even stopped going to the men's breakfast at church. That's because Dale Hinshaw, the head trustee, complains about all the work that needs doing around the place, and Sam ends up spending the day fixing the plumbing or waxing floors or painting a Sunday school room.

So he's stopped going.

The interesting thing is, the less time Sam spends at church, the deeper his faith grows. It kind of troubles him. He's spent nearly fifteen years of his life encouraging people to be active in church so their belief in God would prosper. Then he finds that the less time you spend with the likes of Dale Hinshaw, the easier it is to believe in a gracious God.

So Sam took his children sledding at the park instead. He sprawled across the sled with Levi and Addison piled on top of him. Charlie Gardner pushed them off. What a thrill! Hurtling down the hill, the cold air stinging their faces, leaning to the right to miss the oak tree, then onto the basketball court, which the fire department had sprayed with water and was now covered with ice. They whooshed across the court and slowed to a stop underneath the Lester Worrell Memorial Tree.

The boys jumped off the sled, eager for another ride. Sam rolled off and lay on his back, looking into the sky. The snow had stopped. The sky was blue. It was crisp and cold. The veiny branches of the Lester

Worrell Memorial Tree swayed gently in the north wind.

Such beauty.

It takes about eight inches of snow to make the town beautiful, to cover the junk people leave sitting out in their yards — the old engine blocks and piles of lumber and broken toys and clay pots holding the carcasses of last summer's plants.

Thank you, Lord, for all this beauty and for my sons. Sam's finding it easier to pray now. Every now and then, prayer just wells up within him.

Dale Hinshaw was down at the church, waiting for someone to come in and cook the men's breakfast, but it didn't look like anyone was going to show up. He wondered if they'd cancelled it because of the snow and maybe forgot to call him. The meetinghouse walks needed shoveling. He called over to Sam's house, but Barbara said he'd taken the boys sledding.

"Tell him he needs to stop by and shovel the sidewalks," Dale said. "And he needs to put down some salt too. We're out of salt here at the church, but he can get some at the hardware store."

"I don't think he's going to the meetinghouse today," Barbara said. "He's taking the day off to be with the boys. You'll need to find someone else to clean the walks."

Dale hung up the phone.

It had never been this way with Pastor Taylor. Dale never had to tell him to shovel the church walks; he just knew to do it.

Boy, they don't make preachers like they used to, Dale thought.

He found the shovel behind the furnace downstairs and began shoveling the walk. He rested every five minutes, worried about having a heart attack. He's been getting cramps in his leg at night. He thinks it might be his heart. He's thinking of giving up bacon and trying to get a little exercise, maybe easing up on the Scripture egg project a little bit.

The pressure's been getting to him. The week before, Channel 5 had interviewed him about his Scripture eggs. They filmed him down in his basement, where he's been keeping the chickens. He's up to twenty chickens, which are laying over a hundred eggs a week. He's passed out Scripture eggs to all the Jehovah Witnesses, Unitarians, and Mormons within fifty miles, and is thinking of moving on to the Episcopalians, who are a little too liberal to suit Dale.

He's been doing all the egg distribution himself and is getting tired. He was hoping the interview would generate some volunteers, but no one's called yet.

Way back in August, the elders had promised Dale ten thousand dollars for his Scripture egg project, but so far Dale hasn't seen a dime of that. His wife had been complaining about the chickens being down in the basement, so he was going to use the money to build a coop in his backyard and take the project worldwide. But at the November elders' meeting, Miriam Hodge had persuaded the rest of the elders to reconsider not only their support of the Scripture egg project, but also their decision to build a gymnasium onto the meetinghouse.

Dale's last, best hope was that someone might see him on Channel 5 and send him enough money for the project to go forward. He'd even rented a post office box, which the lady announcer read as they showed the number on the screen. Dale has walked to the post office every day since and peered through the little window, but so far no checks have come.

He doesn't understand why Jessie and Asa Peacock haven't helped. "You'd think with all that money they got, they'd want to help," he grouched to his wife.

He thought about it while cleaning the meetinghouse walks. It was his turn to preach the next day. He decided to preach on the Scripture text, about how those who help a prophet receive a prophet's reward. He thought that would be just the inducement Jessie and Asa needed to part with ten thousand dollars.

He finished shoveling, went home, and spent the rest of the day at the dining room table working on his sermon.

Dale Hinshaw woke the next morning, showered, shaved, and combed back his hair, then ate a little breakfast and put on his black suit. He and the missus drove to church. The streets were plowed smooth. The sun was out, and the snow was melting. Patches of asphalt were showing through. It was the Sunday before Christmas, so there was a big crowd at church.

Ordinarily the sermon comes last in the service. They start with a hymn, then move into prayer time, then take up the offering, then sing another song, then have a little dab of silence in honor of their Quaker heritage. Then there's a fifteen-minute sermon followed by a closing prayer, and they're out the door and eating pot roast within the hour.

But that morning Dale started off with his sermon on how those who help a prophet receive a prophet's reward, then had thirty minutes of silence.

He'd told his wife, "I want to give the Lord sufficient time to convict Jessie and Asa of their sin."

He peered at Jessie and Asa the whole while, but they didn't budge. He kept waiting for one of them to stand and say, "We have a prophet right here in our midst whom we've failed to help. We need to repent of our selfishness and be generous."

Then he would be a magnanimous prophet and forgive them, but not before describing his need — ten thousand dollars to build a chicken coop and take the Scripture eggs worldwide. Then he'd call the ushers forward to take up a special offering. He'd warned Ellis Hodge and Harvey Muldock to be ready with the plates.

But no one stood to speak during the silence except for Wayne Fleming.

"I'd like to ask your prayers for Sally," he said. "We're going to the hospital in a couple weeks to meet with the doctors."

He sat down.

Darn that Wayne Fleming. He's always thinking about himself, Dale fumed to himself. He was going to stand and redirect their attention to his message, but before he could, Miriam Hodge rose to speak.

"I know we've never done this before," she said, "but I'd like for us to gather around Sally and pray for her."

All around the meeting room, people looked at one another, watching to see who'd move first.

Sam and Barbara were the first to move. They stood up in the fifth pew and walked two pews back to where Wayne and Sally and the kids were seated. Uly Grant was right behind them, with Fern Hampton bringing up the rear.

What's going on here? These people are out of control, Dale Hinshaw thought. We're supposed to be praying for my Scripture egg project and taking up a special offering. What's going on here?

He was about to tell people to sit back down, and would have except that Miriam had begun to pray for Sally. It was a radiant prayer. When Miriam finished, Sally and Wayne were crying. Uly passed Wayne his handkerchief, and Fern sat next to Sally and drew her close.

People were crowded thick around the Fleming family. The men were sniffing hard, and the women were weeping. The small children looked on, mystified.

"I know this is unusual," Fern said, "but I'm thinking maybe we should take up a special offering, right now, for Wayne and Sally."

"That's a wonderful idea," Jessie Peacock exclaimed.

Ellis Hodge and Harvey Muldock were poised at the back, offering plates in hand. They moved forward and worked their way through the swarm of people.

They collected over ten thousand dollars. Ellis and Harvey counted it three times on the table in front of the pulpit. People gasped when Ellis announced the total. He had to say it twice. It was mostly neatly folded one-hundred-dollar bills men had pulled from the deep recesses of their worn wallets. Emergency money. Money in case they were up in the city and their car broke down. Jessie and Asa had topped it off with a check for six thousand dollars.

Ellis put the money in a coffee can from the kitchen and handed it to Wayne. Wayne could barely whisper a thank-you.

Dale Hinshaw wanted to snatch the can from Wayne's hand. He thought of taking another collection while people were in a giving mood, but folks had already begun filtering out of the meetinghouse.

As the crowd thinned, Deena Morrison made her way to Wayne and Sally. She sat beside Sally and offered her hand.

212

"Hi, Sally. I'm Deena."

"I know," Sally said, smiling. "My children told me all about you. They really love you."

"They're wonderful children."

"Thank you for being nice to my family while I was gone. You were a real help to them. I hope we can be friends."

"I'd like that." She leaned into Sally and hugged her. "If I can do anything at all, if you need any help, please let me know."

"Thank you, Deena. I will."

Katie climbed onto Deena's lap, and Deena drew Katie to her. "And how are you, Miss Katie?"

"I'm fine, Deena. I miss you. You want to feel my wing buds?"

Deena touched Katie's shoulder blades. "Oh, Katie, those are the finest wing buds in the world."

"You really think so?"

"Yes I do, sweetheart."

Deena looked across Sally to Wayne. "Hi, Wayne. How are you holding up?"

He could still barely talk. He nodded his head. "Gonna be all right." There was an awkward pause. "Your grandmother told me you were thinking of moving back to the city to be a lawyer."

"I've been offered a job, but I haven't

213

made up my mind whether to take it. I'm leaning toward staying."

"I'm glad to hear that. You sure are a blessing to this town."

"I just don't understand this church," Dale Hinshaw complained to his wife as they walked down the aisle toward the door. "I gave them an opportunity to do the Christian thing, and they just sat there like lumps on a log."

"Not everyone has your servant heart, honey."

Dale sighed a heavy sigh. "I'm not sure how much longer I can keep it up. The pressure's getting to me."

"It's more than any one man should have to bear."

They opened the door of the meeting-house. It was dazzling bright. The snow had thawed from the streets. They could hear the *drip, drip, drip* of the melted snow falling from the roof. They walked down the sidewalk.

"What hurts most of all is Asa and Jessie not helping me," Dale said.

"Well, honey, some folks just think only of themselves. That's just the way it is."

Eighteen

A Ministry of Availability

New Year's Day was two weeks past, and most of the people in Harmony had already forgotten their resolutions. Except Sam Gardner, who had resolved to believe in God as quickly as possible so he wouldn't have to listen to the elders preach any more than was necessary.

Harvey Muldock had given one good sermon on how autumn is the season of dying, but that spring brings new life and thus is God's encouragement for us to remain faithful in the face of death. Now that the church had learned of Sally Fleming's leukemia, Harvey's words seemed eerily prophetic.

The second Sunday of January, Harvey preached about how tired the disciples must have been walking on the road to Emmaus. He talked about what a blessing the automobile was and how, speaking of automobiles, Harvey Muldock Plymouth was gearing up for its annual tax sale.

Sam fidgeted in the fifth pew. The preaching was growing worse. The elders

215

were starting their third round of sermons. It was Sam's theory that most folks had at least one good sermon in them and, if pressed, could possibly come up with two. But to hope someone might deliver three good sermons in a row was stretching it. Sam was trying to determine which was better: a bad sermon by someone who believed in God or a good sermon by someone who didn't.

Fern Hampton had given two sermons about Brother Norman's shoe ministry to the Choctaw Indians. In the first sermon she told how in the old days the Choctaw Indians didn't need shoes because they were one with nature. "But then we came along and they adopted our customs, one of which was wearing shoes. Now I figure since we got them started wearing shoes, the least we can do is shod them."

The ladies of the Friendly Women's Circle nodded their heads in solemn agreement.

Fern's second sermon was based on the premise that if you give an Indian a pair of shoes he will have shoes for a year, but if you teach an Indian to make shoes he will have shoes for a lifetime. She wants the Circle to travel to Oklahoma and teach the Choctaws how to make their own shoes.

Miriam Hodge has been the only ray of sunshine amidst this theological drizzle. On the Sundays she preaches, all the rows are filled. She's not a yeller. She doesn't even stand at the pulpit. She stands in the aisle near the first row of pews and speaks from her heart. One Sunday she revealed how she'd been mad at God for not giving Ellis and her any children. People aren't accustomed to this kind of openness. It intrigues them. Except for Dale Hinshaw, who chastised Miriam for being angry with God. But the rest of the people are captivated with her candor. When Dale speaks they think about their pot roast cooking in the oven, but when Miriam speaks they think about their walk with the Lord.

She's been especially helpful to Wayne and Sally Fleming. She goes to the trailer on Wednesday evenings to pray with Sally. Then, on the Sunday before Sally was to begin her treatment, in the quiet after the Harvey Muldock automobile sermon, Miriam had the church pray for the Flemings.

She'd read in the book of James about elders anointing the sick with oil. They'd never done that at Harmony Friends Meeting before, so Miriam reasoned it was a good time to start. She went to the Coffee

Cup and borrowed a bottle of olive oil from Frank Toricelli, who's been using it on Italian Night.

She didn't tell the other elders, for fear it would launch a three-hour debate on the healing properties of olive oil versus those of corn oil. After Harvey spoke, Miriam rose up from the fourth row and invited the elders to gather around Sally. For once, they didn't hesitate or look at one another to see who would go first. They just stood up, walked over to Sally, and put their hands on her head, while Miriam dabbed olive oil on Sally's forehead and prayed for her.

Sally sat there, scarcely moving, not sure what to do. She'd heard of miraculous healings before. She'd seen people talk about it on TV. The people had always felt warm and tingly. She didn't feel that way, though it was nice to be the object of prayer. She's never had this much love directed her way.

When she was a little girl and her mother died, there had been a flurry of concern for her. But after a time people moved on to other cares. She would come home from school to their silent house and lock the door. It was frightening to be so little and by herself, so she'd pretend her mother was alive and in the house with her, taking a nap in the back bedroom. Sometimes Sally would talk to her. Around six o'clock her father would pull up at the broken curb from his job at the factory. Sally would heat up TV dinners in the oven, and they'd sit in front of the television and watch the news. He'd fall asleep on the couch and she'd cover him with a blanket. Then she'd clean the kitchen, do her homework, and go to bed.

She wasn't really raised; she just kind of grew up.

It troubles her to no end that that might happen to her children.

She talked about it with Miriam one Wednesday night in early January after prayer. Wayne was at work, and the kids were in bed. Miriam and Sally were seated on the worn couch.

Miriam had asked Sally, "What can I do for you?"

"Just pray for me."

"Of course I'll pray for you. But is there something else I can do for you?"

Sally began to cry. "If something happens to me, can you make sure my kids are taken care of? Wayne'll have his hands full."

"If anything happens to you, Ellis and I will make sure your children are well cared for. You have my word."

Miriam thinks maybe this is God's reason

for not giving her and Ellis children of their own — so they can care for other people's kids. They call it their "ministry of availability." They took in Amanda, Ellis's niece, the year before. It's been such a joy to have Amanda in their lives. Except they worry that Ellis's no-good brother, Ralph, will sneak back and steal her away, so they've hired the lawyer Owen Stout to begin adoption proceedings. They drive Amanda to and from school and lock their doors at night, just in case. They'd never locked their doors before, on account of Ellis's parents lost the key in 1957. Now, Ellis has put a new lock on the door. It troubles him, having to guard against his own flesh and blood.

The Monday Wayne and Sally went to have tests run at the hospital in the city, Miriam went with them. Ellis stayed home to care for Amanda, and Deena Morrison took the Fleming kids to her house.

The tires are bad on Wayne's truck, so Miriam drove them in hers. She arrived at their trailer a little after seven in the morning. Deena pulled up behind her to take the kids to school. Sally kissed her kids good-bye.

"Will you be home tonight, Mommy?" Katie asked.

"I'm not sure, honey. It depends on what all they have to do. But I promise I'll be home soon. Before you know it."

"Will you be all better then?" asked Adam.

"You bet," Sally said, but to herself she prayed, Oh, dear Lord, please let me live. Please heal me. Let me see my children grow.

They finished their good-byes, then Miriam, Wayne, and Sally climbed into the truck and drove east toward the city. The traffic was light. It was an overcast winter morning. The weatherman on Channel 5 had predicted snow later that day. It took two hours to reach the hospital. Miriam dropped Wayne and Sally off at the front door, then went to look for a parking space.

Wayne and Sally sat on a bench inside the door. It felt good to sit. Sally's been so tired lately. Her appetite has dropped off, and she's been losing weight.

Miriam came through the door. They read the directory on the wall and made their way to the doctor's office. They were right on time for their appointment. Miriam sat in the waiting room while Wayne and Sally talked with the doctor.

They'd met the doctor when they'd come for tests the month before, a Dr. Kinnan. He looked impossibly young to be a doctor, which didn't boost Wayne's confidence.

"Come in. Sit down," the doctor said. "Good to see you again."

"Thank you, Doctor," Wayne said, helping Sally to a chair.

Dr. Kinnan looked at Sally. "How are you feeling?"

"I think I'm doing okay."

"She's been awfully tired," Wayne said.

"Is that right?"

"Yes," Sally said. "Here in the past month or so. I've also not been eating much. I feel full all the time."

"Sally, I need you to sit here on the edge of the table," the doctor instructed.

He probed her stomach and frowned.

"Sally, the reason you feel full is because your spleen is enlarged. This verifies the tests we've been running. It appears your leukemia is advancing. You have what is known as chronic myelogenous leukemia. Fortunately, it is treatable. Though I'd be a lot more hopeful if you had come to us when it was first diagnosed."

No one spoke for a while. Wayne reached over and took Sally's hand.

"But we're not throwing in the towel yet," the doctor said. "We'll just need to be a bit more aggressive in our approach."

He paused.

"We've been having some success with interferon therapy. Unfortunately for you, it seems to work best in the early stages. It's my opinion that your best chance to beat this is through a bone-marrow transplant."

"What's that?" Wayne asked. "How does that work?"

"Simply put, Sally's bone marrow is making too many white blood cells. So what we'll need to do is kill off Sally's bone marrow with chemotherapy and radiation and replace it with new bone marrow from a suitable donor. But before you make that decision, you need to know three things. Number one, a bone-marrow transplant is a very drastic treatment, and you're going to be very sick. You might even die. You need to be aware of that. Number two, we might not be able to find a suitable donor who matches your tissue type. Do you have any brothers or sisters?"

"No," Sally said. "I'm an only child."

"What about your mother and father?"

"My mother died when I was five. I suppose I could ask my father."

"You'll need to do that very soon, Sally. We'll need to see if he's a match, and we need to do it soon. I'd like to start your treatment as soon as possible."

"What's the third thing you needed to

tell us?" Wayne said.

"Despite our success with bone-marrow transplants, many insurance companies still consider it an experimental treatment and won't pay for it. If that's the case with you, you'll need to be able to pay the hospital up front."

"How much would the hospital need?" Wayne asked.

"Around a hundred thousand dollars."

Wayne and Sally didn't speak for several moments.

"It looks like I'm going to die then," Sally said. "There's no way we can come up with that kind of money."

"There'll be other costs, of course, but that's what the hospital will need before admitting you as a patient," Dr. Kinnan explained.

"It might as well be a million dollars," Wayne said.

"Let's not give up yet," the doctor said. "Check with your insurance. You might be surprised."

He stood from his chair, shook hands with Wayne, then turned to Sally.

"I know I've painted a pretty grim picture. But actually, if we get on this now, your odds are even. Fifty percent of the folks who have bone-marrow transplants are alive eight years later. And the odds are inching up all the time. The fact that you're so young is in your favor too. We're going to hope for the best. Okay?"

He patted Sally's arm.

"Thank you," she said, sniffing.

"The nurse is going to come in now and give you information about bone-marrow transplants. She'll also give you some pamphlets to give to your father. Let's be praying he's a match."

Wayne moved next to Sally and put his arm around her.

Dr. Kinnan continued, "We can't afford to wait to see what the insurance company will do. We need to be ready. Time is precious. Right now we're going to extract a small amount of your bone marrow to type it. They're all ready for you down in oncology."

"Then what'll happen?" Sally asked.

"Then you can go home and sleep in your own bed tonight. Remember, though, you need to have your father get in touch with me as soon as possible."

"I'll call him just as soon as I get home."

It was a quiet drive back to Harmony later that day. They stopped for supper outside the city, then drove toward home. The clouds were stacked up in the north, and it was beginning to snow. Fat, wet flakes.

"I wish it was spring," Sally said, breaking the silence. "I wish it was spring and the flowers were blooming and I knew everything was gonna be okay."

Miriam almost told Sally not to worry, that she'd be fine. But she didn't because she wasn't sure. She wasn't sure how this healing business worked. You anoint someone with oil and have the elders pray, and sometimes it works and sometimes it doesn't.

Instead, she reached over and laid her hand on Sally's knee and said, "Well, Sally, whether things work out or not, you are loved."

Outside the truck, the snow was falling faster. The windshield was clouding over. Miriam turned up the heater and shifted down a gear.

Wayne commented on the snow, then fell silent.

The only sound was the thump of the tires on the road joints.

"I tell you one thing," Sally said after a while. "Life sure has a way of making a person pray."

Nineteen

Refreshed

"No," Sam yelled from his bed. "You can't make me go to church."

"Hey, buster, if I have to go and listen to Dale Hinshaw preach, you do too," Barbara yelled back from downstairs. "Now get your carcass out of bed and get down here. Breakfast is ready."

Sam groaned, threw back the covers, and plodded downstairs. Barbara and the boys were seated at the table. They stared at him.

"You look terrible, Daddy," Levi said.

"I don't feel well. In fact, I think I'm too sick to go to church. Yes, that's it. I'm sick."

"You're not sick, and you're not staying home. You're going to church and suffering with the rest of us," Barbara said.

Sam sighed. He'd been doing a lot of sighing lately.

The Thursday before, at the January elders meeting, he had suggested they invite other persons in the church to preach. "Variety is the spice of life," he'd said.

"Sorry, Sam, but I don't agree. What folks need now is preaching straight from

227

the Word. It's bad enough with you not believing in God. We can't risk someone else standing up there misleading folks," Dale Hinshaw said. "Tell you what, don't give the preaching another thought. I'll preach every Sunday from here on out until Sam comes to his senses."

The elders were speechless at the prospect of Dale in the pulpit every Sunday. They hesitated a little too long.

"Well, then, that settles it. I'll start this Sunday."

He preached on his Scripture egg project, how the Lord was using it to correct those in error.

He'd sent a custom Scripture egg to the pope several weeks before. Matthew 23:9: *Call no man your father on earth, for you have one Father, who is in heaven.* He'd hardboiled the egg so it wouldn't break in the mail. Then he'd wrapped it in newspaper, put it in a box, and mailed it off. He's been watching the news ever since for an announcement from the pope.

He wasn't sure how it would happen, but he thought the pope might simply step out on his balcony and, when the people waved and called him Holy Father, would smile and say, "You can call me Johnny."

But so far it hadn't happened. The Scripture is so indisputable Dale was certain the pope would heed it, but he suspected the priest in charge of the mailroom had kept the egg from the pope. Dale conjectured about it during his sermon.

"They probably just let the pope see the nice letters the old ladies send. That's how error continues. The one guy with the power to change things never hears the criticisms."

He went on to encourage the congregation to be open to criticism, then revealed that he had more Scripture eggs to distribute to certain church members in need of correction. After his sermon, he walked down into the congregation and gave an egg to Miriam Hodge, an egg to Sam, and one to Jessie and Asa Peacock.

"Don't let Satan close your ears to reproof," he cautioned them.

That was the third Sunday in January and people were losing their patience. They wanted Sam back in the pulpit.

The week before, Miriam Hodge had stopped him after church and pointed out that nowhere in Scripture does it explicitly state that Quaker pastors must believe in God in order to preach.

"Read your Bible," she told him. "You'll

not find the word *Quaker* in there. I've checked."

The truth is, Sam's heart is being stirred. He mentioned during the elders meeting that he was able to pray again. "I can't quite explain it. I find myself praying more and more. It's been a real blessing."

He asked the elders, "Can we adjust my workload? Sixty hours a week is too much. I think that's what broke me."

When he first came there, the church had given him a list of shut-ins to visit every month. People too tired and sickly to come to church. But those same people felt good enough to visit the Coffee Cup and go on bus trips to the casino in Illinois. Sam told the elders he wasn't going to visit the tired anymore. He said, "These people get out more than I do. I'm the one who's tired. They should visit me."

He figures not visiting the tired will save ten hours a week.

He also doesn't understand why he has to attend every committee meeting. "I didn't go to seminary to help the trustees decide whether the meetinghouse needs painting," he groused to the elders.

The meetinghouse needs to be painted, but Dale Hinshaw won't agree to have it done unless they use paint from Canada that has lead in it. Dale thinks the paint companies bribed Congress to remove lead from paint so it wouldn't last as long and people would buy more paint.

Not going to meetings will save Sam another ten hours a week.

"I grew discouraged because the things I was doing weren't all that important. If I could just minister to hurting people, it might help my faith," he explained to the elders.

So he's been helping people. He assisted the Friendly Women's Circle with the "Help Sally Fleming!" bake sale. To no one's surprise, Wayne Fleming's insurance doesn't pay for bone-marrow transplants — so the Friendly Women have been hard at work raising a hundred thousand dollars.

Since plans to build the church gymnasium were on hold, Sam was a bit mystified why the church couldn't just give the Flemings the money they needed. The church still had the Peacocks' three-hundred-and-fifty-thousand-dollar tithe, after all. He was going to say something about it, but changed his mind after talking with his wife.

She said, "You've been complaining that they never do anything. Now they're trying to do something. Let 'em do it."

So Sam kept quiet.

The Friendly Women taped pictures of Sally and Wayne and the kids on mayonnaise jars, which they've put all over town next to cash registers. A Friendly Woman is stationed at each jar. She frowns at people until they drop in their change.

The "Help Sally Fleming!" bake sale was held on Saturday morning at the bank. The ladies worked all week baking cookies and pies. They met in the meetinghouse basement and made noodles to sell. They rolled out the noodles and Sam cut them, using the sacred noodle cutter, which is stored in a locked cabinet over the sink along with the sacred rolling pin.

Fern Hampton's mother had purchased three rolling pins, two meat-tenderizing mallets, and three noodle cutters at Kivett's Five and Dime in 1964, the year of the first annual Chicken Noodle Dinner. They're down to one of each, the sacred remnants from that celebrated year. Time has sanctified them. Fern washes and dries them and returns these priceless icons to their plywood vault. She carries the key to the cabinet on a chain around her neck.

Early Saturday morning, they loaded the baked goods in Fern's Impala and drove to the bank. Vernley Stout unlocked the door and let them in. They arranged the cookies, pies, and noodles on folding tables flanking the door. To get in the bank you had to pass the Friendly Women. It was an ecclesiastical shakedown.

The farmers drive into town to do their trading. They drop their wives off at the Kroger, then stop in at Kyle Weathers's barbershop to get their hair cut. From there they go to the Co-op on the south edge of town next to the lumberyard. Then they meet their wives back at the Kroger and walk across the street to the bank to pay down their farm loans.

Fern didn't even ask them if they wanted to buy something. She blocked their path, pointed to the pies, and said, "What would you like to buy this morning?"

The farmers complained to Vernley Stout, and he came over to tell Fern she shouldn't harass people.

She glared at him. "So, Vernley Stout, have you always opposed the work of the Lord or is this something new?"

She said it in a loud voice. The Friendly Women looked at Vernley, frowning.

Vernley slunk back to his office and closed the door behind him.

Sam was the cashier. Farmers would count out wrinkled dollar bills into his hand. He'd hand them their change just as Opal Majors, holding a mayonnaise jar, appeared at their elbows and declared, "Your change might be the difference between life or death."

It was amazing how many people donated their change. Sam was thinking of having the Friendly Women's Circle collect the offering at church.

It was such an encouragement to Sam to see the church ministering to someone. It spurred his faith. At the start of the sale, as the ladies unloaded the pies from Fern's car, he'd offered to say a prayer.

They looked at him, startled.

"Sure, Sam. That would be fine," Miriam Hodge said.

He thanked God for meaningful work and asked Him to bless the Friendly Women as they ministered to Wayne and Sally and the kids.

When Sam finished praying, Fern said, "Well, if you can pray, I don't see why you can't preach."

"Maybe before too long," Sam promised.

Sam believes he might be ready to go back in the pulpit. The Lord has been leading him again, just like in the old days. He thinks God might be girding his loins for

Sally Fleming's struggle.

He told Barbara, "In times of trial, doubt is a luxury. Sally can't afford my theological crisis. I need to get on the stick."

Since the first of the year, Sam's been waking up at six o'clock, showering and eating breakfast, then walking to the meetinghouse. He sits in the fifth row for an hour. He prays for Sally and for sick people everywhere. Some mornings he reads his Bible, but mostly he just sits quietly, waiting for God to speak to him.

"Here I am, Lord," he says. "Tell me what you would have me do today. I'm your man."

A little before eight, he hears Frank the secretary swing open the door and step into the meetinghouse. At five after, he smells the coffee brewing. He rises up out of the pew and goes to Frank's office to drink coffee and visit.

They used to begin their day with Frank telling Sam his schedule for the day, but now Sam won't let him. He believes God is telling him to be flexible, to be free to respond to divine prompting. He's told Frank to clear his schedule.

"If anyone calls wanting me to do something, tell them I'll pray about it," Sam instructed him.

"Well, that's one way to lose your job, I suppose," Frank said.

The next Sunday Dale preached his sermon about the pope. Miriam Hodge stayed after church to talk with Sam.

"You seem to be doing better," she said. "Or am I imagining things?"

"I am doing better. I don't know how to describe it, but I feel at rest. I'm slowing down and waiting to see what the Lord wants to do with me."

Miriam smiled. "That sounds peaceful."

"I tell you one thing, it seems a whole lot smarter than trying to impress the Lord with my busyness."

Miriam paused, then spoke from memory. "Come to me, all who labor and are heavy laden, and I will give you rest."

Sam chuckled. "I remember when I was in seminary and had to take a class in Greek. I've forgotten most of it except for that one verse. Matthew 11:28. The word they used there for 'rest' also means 'refreshed.' I think that's the word for how I feel: refreshed."

"I'm glad for you, Sam. And the timing couldn't be better. Quite frankly, I don't think I can take another one of Dale's sermons."

Sam laughed. "Did you open the egg he gave you?"

"Yes, I did."

"What'd it say?"

"He quoted the verse from Paul telling women to be silent in church."

Sam chuckled. "You know, Miriam, I bet Paul would never have written that if he'd known you."

"Thank you, Sam."

What a gifted servant of the Lord, Sam marveled to himself. Lord, thank you for pouring out your Spirit on your people.

"Who's going to tell Dale his preaching days are over?" Sam asked.

"Well, seeing as how women should be silent in church, I think maybe you should tell him."

"I'll have Frank the secretary tell him. He's been to war. He's accustomed to conflict."

"Sounds like a plan," Miriam said.

They walked outside together. Miriam climbed into the truck with Ellis and Amanda. Sam and his family walked toward home. It was a beautiful winter day. They could smell the woodsmoke curling out of the chimneys.

"Hey, Daddy, could you please pretty please take us sledding at the park?" Levi asked.

"Sure. We'll go right after Sunday dinner."

"I hope I don't hurt my hubcap like I did last time," Addison said.

"Honey, it's not your hubcap. It's your kneecap. And I'm sure you'll be fine," Barbara said.

"I hope so. There's nothing worse than a hurt hubcap."

Barbara turned to Sam. "What did the Scripture egg say that Dale gave you?"

"I don't know. I threw it away. I didn't want to hear his criticism."

Barbara laughed and took his arm. "Sam Gardner, you're getting more like the pope every day."

Twenty

The Smallest Good

The phone rang as Jessie Peacock was carrying in the groceries on a Saturday in early February. She set the groceries on the counter and picked up the phone. "Hello."

"I'm looking for a Mrs. Jessie Peacock," a woman's voice said.

"This is Jessie Peacock speaking."

"Mrs. Peacock, you don't know me. My name is Norma Baxter and I live up in the city. My husband got transferred in 1974 so we had to move. Before that we lived in Amo."

"I see."

"Do you know where Amo is?"

"It doesn't ring a bell."

"It's right in between Hadley and Stilesville. Maybe you've heard of Hadley. The church there has a big fish fry every year."

"No, I don't believe I've ever heard of Hadley," Jessie said.

"Well, like I said, we live in the city now."

"That's nice."

"Not really. It's awful noisy, and there

are too many cars."

"I'm sorry to hear that."

"I tell you something else. It doesn't smell very nice in the city, either. Boy, what I wouldn't give to smell a little manure every now and then." Norma Baxter sighed.

"I hate to be rude," Jessie said, "but I'm carrying in my groceries and the ice cream's melting. Was there a reason for your phone call?"

"What kind of ice cream?"

"Pardon me?"

"What kind of ice cream is melting?"

"Oh, butter pecan."

"That's my favorite. I knew we'd have something in common."

"Mrs. Baxter, is there a reason you called?"

"Well, yes. I think I might have something that belongs to you."

Jessie thought for a moment. "I haven't lost anything."

"Well, I tell you, this past Christmas, my husband — his name is Orville — bought me a quilt. Well, Orville, he knows how much I love quilts and how much I miss living in the country, so he went and bought me a quilt at a little antique shop here in the city. Paid four hundred and fifty dollars for it! Can you imagine that? I told him that was too much money, but he made me take it anyway. Orville's sweet that way."

Jessie thought her legs were going to give way. She plopped down in a kitchen chair and took a deep breath. "Is it a wedding ring quilt?"

"It is."

"Does it have the initials *J.L.* in the corner?"

"It does."

"Those are my great-grandmother's initials. Her name was Julia Lindley. She made that quilt for my grandmother as a wedding gift." Jessie began to weep.

"There now, honey, dry up your tears. Like I was saying, Orville got me that quilt for Christmas, but I made him take me back to the shop, and the lady there told us how you and your husband had come back to get it, but by then Orville had already bought it. So I guess the reason I called is that I don't feel right having your grandma's quilt, and I thought you might want it back."

"Oh, I do want it back. Yes, I do."

"Well, the thing is, Orville went kind of overboard on the quilt. That's the most money he's ever spent on me. We're not rich people. I just wish I could afford to give it to you, seeing as how it was your grandma's. But if you could maybe pay us back the four hundred and fifty dollars, that would be nice. You wouldn't have to pay it all at once. You can take the quilt and just send me the money as you get it."

"Oh, no. The money isn't a problem. I'll be happy to pay you for it, plus extra for all your trouble."

"It's been no trouble at all," Norma Baxter said.

Orville and Norma Baxter drove out to Harmony the next day. They wanted to see the Peacocks' farm and smell the manure. They pulled in the driveway around one o'clock, just as Jessie was pulling the pot roast from the oven.

Jessie and Asa had gone to church that morning. Sam was back in the pulpit. He preached about the sheep and the goats and the final judgment, which kind of surprised everyone. They thought sure he'd go easy on them his first Sunday back. Damnation is not Sam's usual topic. He told how Jesus will one day judge the nations and how those who helped the needy would be welcomed into heaven and those who didn't would be cast into the devil's fire. It made folks squirm.

The only people not squirming were the Friendly Women, who had been hard at work helping the needy. They'd held three bake sales for the Flemings. Their goal was to raise one hundred thousand dollars, but to date they were ninety-nine thousand, one hundred and fifty-eight dollars short. So Sam laid it on pretty thick.

The only thing holding up Sally's treatments is the money. Sally's father has had his bone marrow tested and is a strong match. Sally had phoned and told him about her leukemia, and he'd come to her as quickly as he could. He's felt guilty all these years that he never did much for his little girl. Now is his chance to redeem himself. He's ready to go.

After Sam's sermon, Sally stood during the prayer time and told about her father being a good match. All across the meeting room, people smiled. They've been following the Sally Fleming drama closely. Fern Hampton has had the church praying for Sally every day. She's assigned every family in the congregation a half-hour prayer slot and ordered them to pray for Sally each day during their half hour. There weren't enough people to fill the hours, so Fern is praying the night shift. She sits in her chair in her darkened living room and imagines Sally is well and healed and laughing with her children. Then the sun comes up and she bakes a pie for the bake sale.

Jessie and Asa were talking about Sally as they waited for the Baxters to come with the quilt. They've wanted to give Sally the hundred thousand, but Jessie was afraid if they did, the church would lose its momentum and go back to arguing about whether to add on a gymnasium.

"It's a real quandary," she told Asa. "Sally needs help, but it'll be better if the church does it instead of just us. The church needs to experience how good it feels to make a difference."

Asa was adding up some figures at the kitchen table. "Well, the way I got it figured, it'll take three hundred and fifty-four more bake sales for the church to raise the money. That means Sally won't have the money for another . . . let's see . . . six years and nine months." He set down his pencil. "She's a goner."

Just then Orville and Norma Baxter knocked on the kitchen door.

"Come in, come in," Jessie called out.

The men shook hands and the women hugged.

"My, what a pretty place you have here," Norma said. "It reminds me of the farm I grew up on." She sighed.

"Say, that's a nice barn you got there," Orville observed. "It looks new. What happened to your old barn?"

"It burned," Asa said.

"Oh yeah. How did that happen?"

Asa hesitated. "I'd rather not talk about it."

"I don't blame you one bit. It's probably too painful to think about."

"That's it exactly."

Norma was carrying an avocado Samsonite suitcase. She placed it on the kitchen table, unlocked it with a tiny key, and opened it.

"Here it is!" she cried, pulling the quilt from the suitcase with a flourish.

Jessie held it to her, smelling it. It smelled just like her grandmother. Suddenly, Jessie was six years old again and sleeping in her grandmother's feather bed. Tears welled up in her eyes.

"It smells just like Grandma's house used to," she said.

Norma and Orville Baxter beamed.

"This sure was good of you folks to do this for Jessie," Asa said, his voice husky with emotion. "Can't tell you how grateful we are."

"Well, I just think a body ought to do good whenever they can," Norma said.

"Won't you stay and eat Sunday dinner with us?" Jessie asked. "I just took the pot roast out of the oven."

Norma glanced at Orville, and he gave a little nod.

"We'd be happy to," she said. "It smells wonderful."

Jessie went to the cellar and brought up green beans and corn she'd canned the summer before.

They ate in the dining room, which got used only on special days like Thanksgiving and Christmas and the day you got your grandma's quilt back. After dinner, Jessie made coffee and cut slices of pie. Orville Baxter had two pieces, then leaned back in his chair, and patted his stomach. "The corporation is expanding," he said proudly.

Norma Baxter giggled, and Jessie beamed.

Asa went and got the checkbook from the top drawer of their bedroom chest of drawers. "We want to pay you what you paid, plus a little something extra for all your trouble."

But the Baxters wouldn't take extra money, so Jessie gave them the rest of the pot roast and pie, plus three jars of green beans from the cellar. Then they showed the

Baxters their new barn.

"Pure heaven," Norma sighed.

It came time for the Baxters to leave, and Jessie and Asa waved good-bye from the driveway.

"Come back anytime," Jessie yelled out. Orville tooted the horn good-bye.

Jessie went inside to finish cleaning up from dinner while Asa went to the woodshed and brought in an armful of wood. He built a fire in the fireplace. They didn't do that too often — only on special days like Thanksgiving and Christmas and the day you got your grandma's quilt back.

They sat in front of the fire talking about their day, then about how they could help Sally Fleming.

Asa said, "I know you're worried that us helping Wayne and Sally will hurt the church. But it doesn't have to be that way. Maybe it'll inspire the church. Besides, Wayne and Sally'll need lots of other kinds of help."

"I don't know," Jessie said. "I just wish the Lord would let us know what to do. Maybe give us some kind of sign."

They sat staring into the fireplace. Asa rose from his chair and knelt to poke at the fire. He stayed on his knees by the hearth, thinking. "You know, I think we should call

Sam and talk with him about it."

"That's a fine idea."

Sam was taking a nap on the couch when they called. Barbara nudged him awake. "Telephone, honey."

Sam groaned. "Tell whoever it is I'll call 'em back."

"It's Asa Peacock."

Sam sat up on the couch. "Asa Peacock? He never calls. I wonder what's wrong." He hurried into the kitchen and picked up the phone. "Hello."

"Hi, Sam. This is Asa. Sorry to bother you, but Jessie and I was wondering if we could maybe talk with you? It's important."

"Sure, Asa. You want me to come out there or do you want to meet at the meeting-house?"

"Why not let's meet at the church. We can be there in just a little while," Asa said, then hung up the phone.

"What did Asa want?" Barbara asked.

"He and Jessie need to talk with me." He paused, thinking. "I hope they're not having marriage problems."

Bea Majors was at the meetinghouse, practicing the organ. She saw Sam come in and go into his office, then a few minutes later saw Jessie and Asa slip into Sam's office and pull the door shut.

That's curious, Bea thought. I wonder if Jessie and Asa are having marriage problems . . .

She stopped playing and walked quietly to the office door. Jessie was speaking. Bea could barely hear her. She moved a little closer.

"We don't know what to do," Jessie was saying. "We've talked and we've prayed, but we can't seem to work it out."

They're getting divorced, Bea surmised to herself. I knew having all that money would ruin their lives.

She crept outside and drove home, pondering the hardships of life. You think you know somebody, then this happens. A divorce! Who would have thought it? I think I'll call the Friendly Women so we can be praying for them.

"I understand your concern," Sam said. "And while it would be nice if the church could raise all the money, I don't think it's realistic. It would take too long."

"Six years and nine months according to my figures," Asa said.

"That's a lot of bake sales."

"Three hundred and fifty-four more."

"She's a goner," Sam said, shaking his head. "Well, Jessie and Asa, I'll tell you my opinion. I think people ought to do good whenever they can."

Jessie looked up, startled. "That's exactly what Norma Baxter said. She said folks ought to do good whenever they can."

"Who's Norma Baxter?" Sam asked.

"Orville Baxter's wife," Asa said.

"Oh."

Jessie rose to her feet. "Thank you, Sam. You've helped us more than you know."

"That's why I'm here."

They shook hands, put on their coats, and walked outside.

"Can we give you a ride home?" Asa offered.

"No thanks. I think I'll walk."

It was a little after five o'clock and the sun was setting. The town was closed up. The square was empty. He stopped to look at the pocketknife display in the plate-glass window of the Grant Hardware Emporium, just as he had stood and gazed at it when he was a little boy.

His son Levi has been asking for a pocketknife. He wants to carry it in his pocket and learn to whittle. He's promised not to open the blade unless Sam is around. Sam thinks he might buy him one. After all, life is so fleeting, so tenuous, that if you can do someone even the smallest good, you ought to do it.

Twenty-One

The Caribbean

It's been a busy February in Harmony. The radio station over in Cartersburg, WEAK, held a drawing for a seven-day trip for two to the Caribbean. The raffle was a fund-raiser for Sally Fleming, even though Asa and Jessie had given a hundred thousand dollars to help her cause. Their gift made no difference to the Friendly Women, who are bent on raising funds and won't be stopped. It was Fern Hampton's idea for WEAK to set up a card table at the Kroger, in the produce aisle next to the banana rack, and raffle off a trip to the Caribbean for a dollar a chance.

There was a bit of a scandal when the WEAK disc jockey taped a poster to the banana rack showing a woman in a bikini on the beach. It embarrassed the Friendly Women to have their noble cause tainted by such carnality. The poster wasn't particularly revealing, as the woman was an inch tall and standing behind a palm tree. But as Fern pointed out, it doesn't take much to inflame the passions in February. She took a magic marker and colored a dress on the woman.

Still, the Friendly Women raised quite a bit of money at the WEAK Caribbean Trip Giveaway, on account of most everyone in town bought several tickets. The women have been talking about it down at Kathy's Kut 'N' Kurl. They talk about winning the raffle and going to the Caribbean. They aren't sure they'd take their husbands.

"Why ruin a good trip?" Kathy says.

If one of them wins it, the women have decided they're all going to go. "Maybe then the men will learn who really keeps this town going," Kathy says. "Maybe that's what it'll take for them to appreciate us."

Kathy is thinking of becoming the first woman in Harmony with a hyphenated last name.

Sam Gardner didn't buy a ticket. He's too busy to go to the Caribbean. He's been going to the hospital in the city twice a week to visit Wayne and Sally. Ellis Hodge usually goes with him. They sit in the cafeteria and drink Cokes with Wayne while Sally has her chemotherapy and radiation treatments.

Being men, they don't talk about Sally's illness.

"Yeah," Ellis said to Wayne, "you ought to bring your boy out and come ice fishing sometime soon. Me and Amanda caught a nice little mess of bluegill last week. You ought to come on out sometime."

"Yeah, I'll have to do that one of these days."

They talked about whether the church should build on a gymnasium.

"It's gonna come to a head," Sam said. "Dale Hinshaw and Harvey Muldock won't let it drop. You watch and see. They're just waiting for the right moment."

Then they talked for a while about the Peacocks and how nice it was of them to give Wayne and Sally a hundred thousand dollars. Ellis said, "Well, the way I see it, what's the use of having money if you can't help folks? That's just the way I see it."

They sipped their Cokes.

"Say," Ellis said, "is it true what they're saying about the Peacocks?"

"I don't know," Sam said. "What are they saying?"

"Miriam heard they're coming to you for marriage counseling."

"Not that I know of. But maybe they did and I missed it. I've been kind of distracted lately."

Ellis had read in *Popular Mechanics* about a new electric lawn mower that mows the yard all by itself. They talked about that for a while. Ellis is suspicious of the whole thing. He thinks it can't be trusted.

"What's to keep it from running right over you? You watch and see, there's gonna be lawsuits with this one. I tell you what I'd like to see invented. I'd like to see someone invent a toilet seat that lowers after you're done using it. Amanda and Miriam have been after me something fierce about that. We can put a man on the moon, but we can't invent a toilet seat that lowers on its own. I wonder why that is?"

Then they talked about whether it was a waste of money to go to the moon.

The only thing they didn't talk about was Sally and her leukemia. It's too awkward, them being men, and especially with Sally's husband right there with them. But Wayne appreciates Sam and Ellis visiting nonetheless. He gets lonely. They've given Sally medicine to help with the pain, and it makes her sleep. The nurses come in and talk with Wayne but they're too busy to stay long, so Wayne is always glad to see Sam and Ellis.

Wayne's parents come on Sundays. It makes him uneasy. They hadn't wanted Wayne and Sally to marry. Wayne's mother had said some cruel things to Wayne, and though he's forgiven her, he doesn't like having her around.

One day at the hospital she pulled him aside and said, "Maybe you better stay in touch with that nice girl you were dating, just in case Sally doesn't make it. What was her name? Deanna?"

Wayne wishes they'd stay home.

Sally's father comes on Saturdays. He lives in the next state over. He confided to Wayne, "I wasn't a very good father after Sally's mom died. It kinda threw me for a loop." He sits beside Sally's bed and cries. Wayne never knows what to do. He pats him on the back. He's not sure what to say, so he doesn't say anything — he just pats a little faster.

Dr. Kinnan has said that when Sally finishes with the radiation and chemotherapy, they'll do the bone-marrow transplant. Then Sally will have to be in an isolation room until the new bone marrow takes hold. She could be there for months.

Wayne's taken time off from his job at the Kroger. Jessie and Asa's hundred thousand dollars went straight to the hospital, so Wayne and the kids have been living on the WEAK Caribbean raffle money and the ten thousand dollars the church took up in the special offering the Sunday Dale Hinshaw preached.

Deena Morrison has been staying with

the kids out at the trailer. She works at the Legal Grounds while the kids are in school, then Mabel Morrison takes over the shop. Barbara Gardner goes in on Tuesday and Thursday evenings to help close up. Sam stays home and watches the boys.

The first night they built a fort down in the basement. Sam strung clothesline from the furnace over to the shower stall, and they draped blankets over the line. Sam and the boys eat supper down there on Tuesdays and Thursdays. Guy food. Wienies and beans. One night they even slept down there.

On the third Thursday of February, Sam didn't even go to the monthly elders meeting. He stayed home in the fort with his boys. With Sam gone, Harvey Muldock and Dale Hinshaw resurrected the idea of adding on a gymnasium to the meeting-house. They think Harmony Friends Meeting should sponsor a seminar on church maintenance for church trustees from the central Midwest. "We could hold it here if we had a gym," Harvey pointed out.

Harvey and Dale had come up with the idea during the February men's breakfast. They were the only ones to show. They got to talking about what they might do to attract more men to the church, which was when Harvey had the idea of a seminar featuring the latest in power tools and maybe a lecture by Bob Vila.

A gymnasium, they reason, is the perfect venue for men's ministry. They could shoot some hoops, then Bob Vila could talk about tools and home repair. Then Dale, carrying through on the home repair theme, could talk about our Father's many mansions. Dale believes someone has to take care of those mansions — caulk the windows, scrape the paint, and plug the roof leaks. He thinks the church trustees should be prepared.

"So the gymnasium isn't really for us," Dale told the elders. "What we're really doing is equipping folks to serve the Lord into eternity."

Harvey nodded his head in solemn agreement.

When Miriam Hodge told Sam about it the next day, he was glad he'd stayed home to eat wienies and beans in the basement with his boys.

Barbara looks forward to Tuesdays and Thursdays at the Legal Grounds. She goes in at five and doesn't get home until around nine. She likes it that Mabel doesn't talk about the church. They talk about books they've read and world affairs.

All her married life, Mabel had voted a straight Republican ticket under orders from her husband, Harold, proprietor of the Morrison's Menswear shop. But ever since he died, she's been reading books about Harry Truman and the Kennedys. She even took down the framed picture of Richard Nixon that had hung in their living room since 1968.

"Don't get me wrong," she told Barbara one Tuesday night, "I miss Harold, but I always felt I lived in his shadow. It wasn't easy being married to a pillar of the community."

"Don't I know it. You should try being married to a minister. People think the only thing you can talk about is church. And it's all Sam talks about. Are all men like that?"

"My Harold was. Everything revolved around the shop. We never even went on vacation. We'd go to the annual International Shoe Company customer appreciation dinner in St. Louis. Twenty-one years straight. It's the only place I've ever been." Mabel sighed.

Barbara patted Mabel's hand. "Maybe you'll win the radio trip to the Caribbean. I'll pray for that to happen."

But she didn't pray too hard, because she wanted to win that trip herself. The only place she's been lately is up to the city to visit Sally Fleming. She and Miriam Hodge drove to the hospital the last Saturday in February. They left the kids at home with their husbands. Barbara said to Miriam, "I know it's Sam's job to visit Sally, but if I was lying in bed throwing up and my hair was falling out in clumps, the last thing I'd want is a bunch of men standing around gawking at me. I wouldn't care if one of them was my pastor."

They stayed a couple hours. They caught Sally up on all the news and told her about the WEAK Caribbean Trip Giveaway. Sally mostly talked about her kids. She hadn't seen them for several weeks. She worried it would frighten them to see her bald, so Wayne had the kids draw her pictures, which Barbara and Miriam thumbtacked to the bulletin board in her hospital room.

It makes Sally cry to look at the pictures. Stick drawings with the words *We love you* written in crooked letters along the bottom. She remembers how she ran away and is wracked with guilt.

"But when that doctor told me I had leukemia, I just wasn't thinking," Sally confided to Barbara and Miriam. "I just felt I had to leave. I couldn't bear the thought of the kids watching me die the way I watched my mother. Then I got to missing them so much I had to come back." She began to cry. "I guess I'm not much of a mother."

"There now," Miriam said, patting her arm. "Don't talk that way. You're a good mother. You were just confused, that's all."

Barbara isn't sure what to think. She talked about it with Miriam on their drive home. "I really like Sally, but I don't see how she could have just left her family like that."

Miriam thought about that for a while, then said, "Well, Barbara, we just never know what we'll do. People do odd things when they think they're going to die. When I had breast cancer, I didn't tell my sister until after it was all over. I just couldn't deal with her knowing." She paused. "You think you know how you'd handle being something, but you don't until it's happened to you."

"I guess you're right. I hope I never have to find out."

"I hope you never have to either, Barbara. I will say one thing, though. When you've survived a bad sickness, life takes on a certain appeal it never had before. It's really hard to have a bad day." Miriam laughed.

"Though I must admit that an elders meeting with Dale Hinshaw can make the grave seem a welcome prospect."

It depressed Barbara to see Sally. It's been a hard year, what with Sam's struggle and everyone talking about him behind his back. She walks into the Kut 'N' Kurl, and the ladies smile and change the subject. Some days she wishes Sam had gone into a different line of work. She's never told him that, but she wishes it just the same.

She's hoping they'll win the Caribbean trip for two. She'd bought ten raffle tickets. She called Sam's brother, Roger, to see if he could watch the kids, just in case.

Barbara even ordered a new bathing suit. The UPS man delivered it the last day of February while the boys were in school and Sam was at work. She tried on the bathing suit and studied herself in the mirror.

Not bad for a woman pushing forty with two kids, she thought. Not bad at all.

She hid the bathing suit in her bottom drawer.

She could use seven days in the Caribbean. She's not sure Sam would even go if they win. She can hear him now: "I don't know, it just doesn't seem right for us to go on vacation, what with Sally in the hospital and all."

But there's always someone in the hospital. There's always a crisis. He complains about the church never giving him a vacation, but the truth is he wouldn't go on vacation if they did give him one. Sam's idea of a vacation is a three-day visit to her parents' house. Even then he calls the church once a day to check with Frank the secretary.

If she wins the trip, she's going — with or without him. She's going to pack her swimsuit and fly to the sunny Caribbean. If Sam won't go, she'll take Mabel Morrison. They'll sit beside the pool, and when the waiter walks past she'll say, "Hey there, buddy, could you pour me another one?"

It's been a long year, and she could use the break.

Twenty-Two

Bea and the Reverend

It was the morning of Ash Wednesday, the first day of Lent, and the Coffee Cup restaurant was full. Vinny was at the griddle flipping pancakes, and Penny worked the booths, pouring coffee. Dale Hinshaw sat at the counter next to Asa Peacock.

"I was wondering if you could maybe look at my chickens," Dale said.

"What's going on?" Asa asked.

"I'm not sure. Their feathers are falling out, and they're not laying as many eggs."

"All the chickens or just some of them?"

"Just some."

"It's probably nothing. A lot of times they'll molt this time of year. As for the egg production, you might try increasing their feed."

"It couldn't have happened at a worse time. I was going to the airport this weekend to pass out Scripture eggs to the Moonies. Now it looks like I'm running short of eggs." Dale sighed. "First the church didn't give me the ten thousand dollars they promised. Now my chickens are looking puny. If I

264

didn't know any better, I'd think the Lord had set His heart against my Scripture egg ministry."

"Now don't go getting all discouraged. Remember, Jonah had his whale and Daniel had his lion's den."

"Maybe it's a test," Dale said.

"I bet you're right."

"Could you and Jessie pray for me?"

"You know we will. Of course, it could be stress. Are you still keeping the chickens in your basement?"

"Yep, at least until I get enough money to build a coop."

"You might try letting them outside every now and then. They like fresh air. You could try taking them for a walk. That might help."

"You think so?"

"Couldn't hurt." Asa stood and plucked his bill from the counter. Vinny rang him up. "Happy Lent," Asa told him.

"Thank you," Vinny said.

"Are the Catholics having church to-night?"

"You bet. What about you guys? Do the Quakers recognize Lent?"

"Not really. We believe people should feel guilty the whole year round, not just for forty days."

Vinny laughed and handed him his change. Asa deposited it in the Help Sally Fleming! pickle jar next to the cash register. Vinny peered at the jar. "How's Sally doing?" he asked.

"Not good. Sam talked about her in church on Sunday. They went ahead with the transplant, and they've got her in isolation. But it looks like she's got some kind of infection. She's fevered."

Vinny shook his head. "Sorry to hear that."

"Maybe you could put her on the prayer chain at your church."

"We're one step ahead of you. She's been on there for a month now. We're keeping a candle lit for her."

"Thank you, Vinny. Times like this, a person needs all the prayer they can get."

Vinny peered at Asa. "Is there anything else we can be praying about? Maybe something of a personal nature for you and Jessie?"

"Not that I know of. But if I think of anything, I'll be sure to let you know."

People have been asking that a lot lately. They've been asking how Asa and Jessie are doing and talking about how marriage is so difficult these days, what with Hollywood winking at infidelity and all.

Asa isn't sure why people have taken such an interest in marriage. The Sunday before, Bea Majors had risen from her seat at the organ during the prayer time and asked Sam if he could pray for all the marriages in the church.

"It just seems to me that Satan is hard at work destroying our marriages," she said from the organ.

People stared at her. Satan doesn't get mentioned much at Harmony Friends, but lately Bea has been dragging him out every Sunday. She's been watching the Reverend Johnny LaCosta of the Johnny LaCosta Worship Center on Wednesday nights after *Jeopardy!*. According to the Reverend Johnny LaCosta, Satan has been working a good deal of overtime.

She talked with her sister, Opal, about it. Opal thinks Johnny LaCosta is a fraud.

"Number one," she told Bea, "don't trust any minister who accepts Visa or MasterCard. And number two, any minister who names a church after himself is a gasbag and a bozo."

Bea thinks Opal is in denial, another thing the Reverend Johnny LaCosta warned about. Bea's thinking of sending the Reverend a little donation so he can get the truth out to more people. A fifty-dollar donation will get her a prayer cloth touched by the Reverend Johnny LaCosta himself.

Jessie Peacock suspects people have been talking about her and Asa, though she isn't sure why. The week before, she had run into Fern Hampton at the Kroger, and Fern had informed her that her nephew Ervin was thinking of becoming a counselor.

"He never really took the classes," Fern explained, "but he's read several books on the subject. He's working for the street department now, so he's only available of an evening." Then she leaned closer to Jessie. "Sometimes it's easier to talk to a stranger."

"I suppose that's true."

Fern slipped Jessie a piece of paper. "Just in case anyone were to ask, here's his phone number." She patted Jessie's hand. "It's nothing to be ashamed of. We all need help every now and then."

Fern blames Jessie and Asa's marriage troubles on the lottery money. She's discussed it at length with Bea. "It was bound to happen," she said. "Money changes people."

Though Jessie and Asa have noticed people acting a little strange, they haven't talked about it with one another. Asa was going to raise the subject with Jessie, but then he found the slip of paper in a grocery bag with *Ervin* written on it, along with a telephone number.

He anguished about it for several days.

Maybe this is what people have been talking about, he thought. Maybe this is what Vinny meant when he asked if Jessie and I needed prayer. Everyone knows but me. It's always the husband who's the last to know.

He finally asked Jessie one night after supper. "Uh, honey, I was just wondering how things are going for you. Are you feeling all right? Is everything okay?"

"Everything's fine. Couldn't be better!"

"Say, by the way, I found this and thought it might by yours." Asa handed her the piece of paper with Ervin's name on it.

Jessie studied the piece of paper, then smiled. "Oh, this is Fern's nephew. He's a counselor. Except that right now he's working for the street department. Fern gave me his number last week at the grocery store."

"Are . . . are you seeing him?"

"Of course not. I don't need counseling." She began to clear the dishes from the table. "It is odd, though. Everyone's been asking me how I'm doing."

"Me too. I wonder if there's something going on we don't know about?"

"Hard telling. The way people gossip in this town, it could be anything."

They talked for a while about what they could do with that month's interest money. Bea Majors has been after Jessie to send money to the Reverend Johnny LaCosta.

"Jessie, it's like he knows your heart," Bea said. "He just stares right out of that TV screen and peers into your soul. Plus, if you give a thousand dollars, he writes your name down in the Book of Life, which he locks in a vault so it'll be safe when the Lord returns. That way the Lord'll know who's been faithful."

Jessie told Asa about Bea as they were washing dishes.

Asa shook his head. "I'm afraid Bea's straw doesn't reach the bottom of the glass."

"Yeah, something's not right there. Speaking of Bea, what was that song she played for the offering this past Sunday?"

"I think it was 'Tiny Bubbles.'"

"Maybe we could use this month's money to hire a new organist for the church."

Asa chuckled.

Instead, Jessie and Asa decided to set

aside more money for Wayne and Sally Fleming. They want to get the Flemings out of that trailer and into a house with a yard so the kids can have a safe place to play. But for now they just want Sally to get well.

Her infection and fever had gotten so bad that Sally had asked to see the kids, so Deena Morrison brought them to the hospital. The doctors let them behind the isolation curtain, but they had to wear masks and gloves.

Deena told Jessie about it after church.

"It was pitiful. The kids were crying. Wayne and Sally were crying. I couldn't bear to watch it."

"What are the doctors saying?" Jessie asked.

"Oh, you know doctors. They won't say one way or the other. But I don't see how she can make it. She's wasting away."

The Friendly Women's Circle met the next Tuesday. They talked about Sally while they stitched their annual fund-raiser quilt for Brother Norman's shoe ministry to the Choctaw Indians.

Bea Majors suggested they load Sally in Harvey Muldock's RV and drive her to the Reverend Johnny LaCosta's healing service. "He could cure leukemia with one hand tied behind his back. I've seen him do it. He can heal just about anything — cancer, consumption, warts."

The Friendly Women want to believe people can be healed — they just wish God would use someone more credible than the Reverend Johnny LaCosta.

"It's his hair," Miriam Hodge complained. "Why does it have to be so big? And what's with the white suit? He looks like Colonel Sanders."

Sam was at the meetinghouse that morning. They asked him what he thought of the Reverend Johnny LaCosta.

"Not much," he told them.

Bea whispered to Fern Hampton, "That's jealousy talking. Sam's been praying for Sally all these months, and nothing's happened."

Back in January, Bea Majors and Dale Hinshaw had written a letter to the Reverend Johnny LaCosta inviting him to preach the June revival at Harmony Friends Meeting. The only thing they got back was a picture of the Reverend with a request for a donation to expand the Johnny LaCosta Worship Center.

Dale sent him ten dollars and asked if he could appear with his Scripture eggs on the Reverend's TV program.

Bea taped the Reverend's picture to her bathroom mirror. It's the first thing she sees every morning.

Johnny LaCosta has never married and neither has Bea. She thinks the Lord might want them together. It's the way he looks at her from the television set, like he knows her heart. She's hoping he'll come to Harmony for the June revival and they'll get together. She sent him a picture of herself playing the organ. She signed the back of the picture *Fondly, Bea.* She was thinking of writing *With Deep Affection,* but didn't want to come on too strong.

The night of Ash Wednesday, she hurried home from Italian Night at the Coffee Cup to watch *Jeopardy!.* Her sister, Opal, watched too. They talked on the phone, guessing the answers and discussing Alex Trebek.

"Except for his hair turning gray and the liver spots, you'd never know he was pushing sixty," Bea said.

At seven twenty-eight she told Opal good night, then flipped over to Channel 40 to watch Johnny LaCosta's *Hour of Truth* program from seven-thirty to eight. It's their time to be alone, to commune soul to soul.

Johnny was talking about Lent and why he was opposed to it. Nowhere in Scripture is Lent mentioned, he pointed out. "We know for a fact that Lent has its origins in a pagan religion from the area of Babylon. We've invited the pope to come on the *Hour of Truth* for a frank discussion of the whole Lenten heresy, but he's declined to meet with us."

He frowned. It appeared to pain the Reverend Johnny LaCosta to have to rat on the pope.

I wonder if Vinny knows this, Bea thought. I'm glad there's someone out there willing to tell the truth.

She rose from her chair and wrote out a check for fifty dollars to the Johnny LaCosta Worship Center along with a note asking him to pray for Sally Fleming. She licked the envelope shut and clothes-pinned it to the mailbox on her front porch.

She's thinking if she gets the prayer cloth in time, she might drive up to the hospital and have Sally touch it. And while she's at it, she might let Asa and Jessie have a go at it too.

Twenty-Three

The Ministry of Noodles

Gosh, I'm getting tired of this. I need a vacation, Bob Miles thought as he sat typing at his desk at the *Harmony Herald.*

He's written "The Bobservation Post" column every Tuesday for nearly twenty years. Twenty years of looking out the front window from eight to nine in the morning and writing what he sees. It's the same thing every week: Jessie Peacock going into the Kroger, Kyle Weathers sweeping his sidewalk, and the lawyer Owen Stout walking with his briefcase past the Coffee Cup. He wishes a tavern would open on the town square. Instead of writing about what went on Tuesday mornings, he could write about what happened on Saturday nights.

Bob leaned back in his chair and imagined such a column:

There goes church elder Harvey Muldock, looking both ways to see if anyone is watching, then slipping into the tavern. Deena Morrison is locking the door to the Legal Grounds. She's

275

walking past the tavern. Ernie Matthews gives a wolf whistle and leers at her.

A smile crossed his face. That'd sure sell some papers.

Instead, he wrote about Jessie Peacock going into the Kroger, Kyle Weathers sweeping his sidewalk, and the lawyer Owen Stout walking with his briefcase past the Coffee Cup.

Bob has been wanting to take the *Herald* in a new direction. He's thinking of adding a liberal columnist to the editorial page. Maybe print a commentary or two in favor of socialized medicine or expanding the welfare system. Maybe something in support of gun control or against prayer in school. Something to get folks agitated. He's been bored lately and could use the excitement.

He'd been keeping a close eye on the Wayne-and-Deena dating dilemma. When Sally came home, Bob had hoped for some kind of fracas to write about. Preferably one in public where he could take photographs of Sally and Deena catfighting over Wayne. But then Deena bowed out of the picture, and there went his story.

"She sure picked the wrong time to be noble," he complained to his wife, Arvella.

"I needed something to liven up the front page."

"Maybe you could write about the Friendly Women and their fund-raiser for Brother Norman's shoe ministry to the Choctaws. People kind of expect that this time of year."

"I was thinking about that. I tell you what I'd like to know. I'd like to know what this Brother Norman character is doing with all the money they've been sending him. There can't be that many shoeless Choctaws."

The next Tuesday he visited the Friendly Women and took a picture of them at the quilting frame in the meetinghouse basement. Underneath the picture he wrote, *The Friendly Women of Harmony Friends Meeting stitch a fund-raiser quilt for Brother Norman's supposed shoe ministry to the Choctaw Indians.*

He passed out the papers Thursday morning, then left for a vacation in Florida. Bob's always wanted to go to Florida, and after Arvella read that week's paper she thought this might be just the time for them to go.

They left that afternoon and made it as far as Louisville.

"We should be safe here," Arvella said, so Bob took the next exit and they stayed the night in a Motel 6. They woke up the next morning, ate breakfast at Bob Evan's, then got back on the Interstate and headed south. It was kind of exciting, being on the run. Every five minutes he'd check his rearview mirror.

"Looks like we made a clean getaway," he announced as they crossed into Georgia.

Back in Harmony, the Friendly Women were worked into a lather. *Supposed* shoe ministry. The nerve of him! They held an emergency meeting in the basement. Fern Hampton demanded they boycott the *Herald*, until it was pointed out that the *Herald* was free in the first place.

"Then let's boycott his advertisers. That'll teach them not to consort with the media elite."

Oh, they were mad. To labor so hard on the Lord's behalf only to be attacked by the liberal press. "It's enough to make a person rethink the First Amendment," Fern fumed.

Opal Majors suggested they hire the lawyer Owen Stout. "Let's sue his pants off. That'll teach him not to mess with the Friendly Women."

It wasn't a pretty sight, what happened in that basement. All their suppressed anger rose to the surface. For months they had avoided contention in order to labor for the common good of Sally Fleming. But you can be good only so long, and the Friendly Women had reached their limit.

They were not only mad; they were discouraged. They'd thought that with all their work, God would bless their efforts by healing Sally.

The next Sunday, after church, they went to see her. They drove to the city and stood peering through the glass into Sally's room as she lay in her isolation tent. Fifteen robust Quaker women bringing all their faith to bear. Sally was asleep, so they clutched about the doorway and watched her. Wayne was there, tired and rumpled. The women lined up to hug him.

"We've been praying for you and Sally," Miriam Hodge said.

"How's she doing?" Fern asked.

"Not good." His throat caught. "The doctors say the new bone marrow they gave her is attacking her body. They call it graft-versus-host disease. I guess it's pretty serious."

Miriam grimaced. "Does Sam know about this?"

"No, I haven't told him yet. I just found out myself this morning." Wayne slumped in the doorway.

"Have you eaten anything today?" Jessie Peacock asked.

"No, I've been sitting with Sally."

"You have to eat. Let's go down to the cafeteria and get you something to eat."

She took him by one arm, Miriam took him by the other. The rest of the Friendly Women fell into formation and marched behind them to the elevator that took them down to the basement cafeteria.

Wayne didn't want to eat, but they made him.

"Clean your plate," Fern ordered.

So he did. He knew better than to argue with the Friendly Women.

"How's Sally been eating?" Jessie asked.

"Not too well. She's lost her appetite. The food here isn't all that good."

"What she needs is some of our chicken and noodles," Fern said.

"Oh, the doctors wouldn't allow that. They don't let you bring in food. They said it could be contaminated."

"Contaminated! I'll have you know no one's ever got sick from my cooking." Fern stood up from the table. "Come on, Friendly Women, we're going to make some noodles."

They fell into formation and marched into the cafeteria kitchen. There were two men in there. One had a naked woman tattooed on his forearm. The other had a ponytail. They had dirty fingernails. They were smoking cigarettes, the ashes falling onto the countertop.

Men! Those Friendly Women had had it up to here with men. First it was Bob Miles impugning Brother Norman's integrity. Now it was these two men with dirty fingernails smoking in a kitchen.

Fern glared at them. "Out! And don't come back!"

It took the Friendly Women four hours to make the chicken and noodles. They sent Jessie to the grocery store to buy a chicken. "I wish I'd brought one with me," Jessie lamented. "Those store-bought chickens are nothing but white lumps of chemicals."

"It'll have to do," Fern told her.

Say what you will about Fern Hampton, when leadership is needed, she's not one to waver.

They carried the chicken and noodles up to Sally's room. She was awake by then. Fern hoisted her up in bed, and Miriam spoon-fed her the noodles. Sally ate half a bowl before falling back to sleep. Wayne ate the rest.

The Friendly Women stood back,

awaiting her revival.

"Lord, raise her up," Mrs. Dale Hinshaw prayed aloud.

But Sally just lay there, pale and worn, her breath a rattle.

"She sounds just like Dale's chickens," Mrs. Dale Hinshaw whispered to Jessie Peacock. "They're not doing so hot either."

They watched Sally another half hour.

"Maybe this is one of those slow miracles," Bea Majors said. "The Reverend Johnny LaCosta was talking about that the other night. He said sometimes God delays your miracle to teach you patience."

"That must be it," Fern agreed.

Wayne had fallen asleep in the chair next to Sally. They filed out of the room and rode the elevator to the ground floor.

It was a quiet drive back to Harmony. It was after dark by the time they pulled in front of the meetinghouse. Miriam could see a light on in Sam's office. She went inside and tapped on his door.

"Come in," he called out.

Miriam pushed open the door. "What are you doing here? Shouldn't you be home with your family?"

"The boys are on spring break this week. I'm working now so I can take a few days off to be with them."

Miriam smiled. "Enjoy them while you're able. Life's a fragile thing."

"Yes it is. Have a seat. Let's talk."

"Thank you, I will. It's been a long day."

"How's Sally?"

"Not any better. The doctors told Wayne this morning that the new bone marrow is starting to attack her body. I guess it's pretty serious."

Sam leaned back in his chair and shook his head.

Miriam continued, "You read all the stories in the Bible about Jesus healing people. With all our prayer, I just don't understand why He isn't healing Sally."

"I've wondered that myself sometimes."

"What do you make of it?"

"Well, I tell you, Miriam, I don't want to say God can't heal. After all, He's God. He can do whatever He wants. But for whatever reason He doesn't seem to do it nearly as often as we ask."

"That's true enough. I wonder why that is?"

"I think it has to do with freedom. God created a free world. And in a free world there exists the possibility not only for beauty and happiness, but ugliness and sorrow."

Miriam sat silent. "I suppose you're right," she said after a while.

"So did you see any beauty today?"

"I did. I saw a bunch of women spend their day comforting Wayne and Sally the only way we knew how."

"How was that?"

She laughed. "We made them noodles."

"And I bet that made them feel loved."

"I hope so." The words caught in her throat. "I hope they know we love them."

"I'm sure they do." Sam paused. "You know, Miriam, maybe God is healing Sally after all, and we just can't see it."

"What do you mean?"

"I mean that sometimes our deepest wounds are the invisible ones, the ones medicine can't heal."

Miriam looked at Sam. "Are you speaking from experience?"

"I am."

"From when you lost your faith?"

"Yes. I'd been praying for God to do something here and when He didn't do what I asked, I lost heart. Then I realized He was doing something, just not what I was asking."

"So because you were looking to Him to do something in one area, you were blind to what He was doing somewhere else."

"Yeah, I guess that's what happened," Sam admitted.

"So what was God doing somewhere else?"

"What God always does. Being lovingly present."

"Forgive me for saying so, but sometimes it feels like that isn't enough. Don't you wish He'd do more?"

Sam chuckled. "Of course I do. Right now I wish God would cure Sally Fleming of leukemia."

"Do you think He could?"

Sam thought for a moment. "I'm not sure. I just don't know."

"Doesn't that drive you nuts, not knowing?"

"Not really. But then I've never thought we can know all there is to know."

Miriam sighed. "It makes me tired to think of it."

"It does me too. Let's go home to our families."

They walked outside. It was dark. The spring peepers were starting up. The light over the meetinghouse door shone down on the daffodil stems just breaking through the ground.

"I'm glad spring's here," Sam said. "It's a lot easier to be optimistic in the springtime."

He saw Miriam to her truck, then walked toward home. It was warm. Easter was nearing.

He thought about Bob Miles stirring up all kinds of excitement and leaving town.

What a luxury to have such a boring life you need to stir up excitement, he thought. I must be getting old. A little boredom sounds good right about now.

Twenty-Four

A Time to Die

Good Friday morning, Sam Gardner and his brother, Roger, sat at the counter of the Coffee Cup eating breakfast. Roger had come home from the city for the Easter weekend. He and Tiffany, the vegetarian, had broken up.

"I couldn't take it anymore," he told Sam. "It was all she talked about — vegetable this and vegetable that. Plus, she was starting to go a little overboard."

"Oh yeah? What'd she do?" Sam asked.

"She started carrying a can of spray paint with her and whenever she'd pass someone wearing a fur she'd spray-paint 'em."

Sam laughed. "You're kidding."

"No, I'm not. She was going off the deep end. She even got put in jail once. But that's not the worst of it. She saw me in the drive-through lane at Burger King. All I ordered was a Coke, but she accused me of fraternizing with the enemy and didn't talk to me for an entire month."

"That's a little extreme."

"All she ever talked about was what she

believed. Never cared what anyone else thought. Never lifted a hand to do anything for anyone, but expected the whole world to bow to her wishes. To tell you the truth, I'm glad to be shed of her."

The bell over the door tinkled. Ernie Matthews walked in. "Hey, Roger, long time no see."

There was an empty seat next to Sam. Dear Lord, please let him sit somewhere else, Sam prayed.

"I'll just sit here next to Sam. You don't mind, do you Sam?"

"Actually, Roger and I —"

"Good, good. I'll just sit right here. Hey, Penny, can you pour me some coffee over here? Say, Sam, I got this joke. You'll get a kick out of this one, you being a minister and all. This man walks into a church and sees all these names written on the wall. The pastor comes up to him, and the guy says, 'What are all these names doing on the wall?'

"The pastor says, 'Those are the names of the people who died in the service.'

"The guy looks at the pastor and says, 'Was that the eight o'clock service or the ten o'clock service?' "

Ernie bellowed and slapped the table.

Lord, how could you do this to me? Sam thought.

"That was pretty good, Ernie," Roger said. "I bet the ladies around here really appreciate your sense of humor. So are you dating anyone now?"

"No, no one in particular. I'm kinda playing the field. But I've been thinking of giving Deena Morrison a chance to date me."

"I bet she can hardly wait," Sam said.

"Who's Deena Morrison?" Roger asked. "I've not heard of her. Any relation to Harold and Mabel Morrison?"

"She's their granddaughter," Sam said. "She moved here last year to open a law practice, but now she's running the Legal Grounds Coffee Shop." He leaned closer to Roger. "She's not dating anyone at the moment. You want to meet her?"

"Not me. I've had it with women."

"You'd change your mind if you ever met her. She's a remarkable lady."

The bell over the door tinkled again. Dale Hinshaw and Asa Peacock walked in and took a booth near the back, underneath the swordfish. Penny poured them coffee, and Vinny dropped four more eggs on the griddle.

Dale sighed.

"What's wrong?" Asa asked.

"It's my chickens. They're losing more feathers than ever."

"Did you try giving them some fresh air like I suggested?"

"Yep, I've taken them on walks every night. Do you know how hard it is to take twenty chickens on a walk? They're not like dogs, that's for sure."

"Gee, Dale, I'm sorry to hear of your troubles."

"Oh, it'll work out okay. I guess I just have to have faith. Speaking of troubles, are you and Jessie doing any better?"

"What do you mean?"

"It's okay, Asa. You don't have to be embarrassed. I know you and Jessie have been having marriage problems. In fact, everyone knows. It's all over town. I just want you to know I've been praying for you."

Asa stared at Dale.

"What happened?" Dale prodded. "You can tell me. Did winning all that money go to Jessie's head? I was afraid that would happen. I tried to warn her in a Scripture egg."

"Dale, I don't know what you're talking about. We're not having marriage problems. We're getting along fine."

Dale reached across the table and laid his hand on Asa's shoulder.

"Now, Asa, I know this is hard for you, but you can be honest with me. How about me and the missus come visit you sometime? Maybe we can share some Scripture and put Satan on the run."

"I tell you, Jessie and me are doing fine."

"All right, if you say so. But I just want you to know that if you need someone to talk with, I'm here for you."

"I'll remember that. I appreciate your concern."

How sad, Dale thought. He can't see what is perfectly clear to everyone else in town. Poor guy.

Asa didn't feel much like eating after that. He pushed his eggs around the plate and drank a little coffee, then excused himself.

"See you tonight at church," he told Dale, then paid his bill and left.

Asa went home and told Jessie what had happened. She was so upset she wanted to cry. "I can't believe they would think that of us," she said. "After all these years, for them to think that about us. How could they? To heck with them. I'm going to the Catholic church tonight. That'll show 'em."

"Now, now, don't get all worked up," Asa said. "They didn't mean anything by it. Besides, if I go to the Quaker church and you

291

go to the Catholic church, they'll really start talking then."

She finally settled down, but it took a while. Asa was glad he had work to do outside.

The Good Friday service began at seven that evening. Sam got there with his family around six-thirty, turned on the lights, and got the coffee going.

The Harmony Friends Good Friday service is always a brief one. They meet for a half hour to contemplate the Crucifixion, then retire to the basement for cookies and coffee. "Why get all worked up?" is their philosophy. "We know things turn out okay in the end."

Roger came with Sam and Barbara and the boys. He's not a big one for the church — never went in for God in a big way — but he likes cookies. He stood next to Sam as people entered the meetinghouse. He saw Deena Morrison walking down the sidewalk with the three Fleming kids. "Say, who's that?" he asked Sam.

"Deena Morrison. But since you're not interested in women, I won't bother to introduce you."

"You didn't tell me she had kids. I like kids."

"Those aren't hers. Those are the Fleming kids. Their mom's the one in the hospital with leukemia. Deena's been caring for them."

"That's awful good of her."

"I told you she was remarkable."

Deena and the Fleming kids climbed the steps. "Hi, Sam," Deena called out.

"Hi, Deena. Deena, this is my brother, Roger. Roger, this is Deena."

Deena smiled at Roger.

Oh, she was beautiful. She was so . . . so . . . robust. She was no Tiffany, that was for sure.

"Are you a vegetarian?" he asked.

She laughed.

Oh, her laugh was a joy.

"No, I'm not a vegetarian. Why do you want to know?"

Dumb, dumb, dumb, Roger said to himself. Roger Gardner, you are a moron.

"Oh, no special reason. I was just curious. Say, it's kind of crowded in our pew. Do you mind if I sit with you? Maybe I could help you with the kids. I really like kids."

Lord, please let her say yes, Roger prayed. Suddenly, Roger Gardner believed in prayer as never before.

Deena smiled. "Sure, you can sit with us."

293

Roger's insides shuddered. Thank you, Lord. I'm your man from here on out.

Roger and Deena sat in the Wilbur Matthews pew, just behind Fern Hampton. The Fleming children sat between them.

Roger was glad his mother had made him change clothes before coming to church. He'd come downstairs wearing black, his favorite color. A black polyester shirt with black pants and black shoes. He was thinking of growing his hair long enough to wear a ponytail.

His father had looked up from his easy chair. "For cryin' out loud," Charlie Gardner had snorted.

For Christmas, a few months before, Roger's mother had bought him a new outfit from the Penney's catalog — khaki pants, a blue shirt, a navy blazer, and a reversible belt. "Didn't you like what we bought you for Christmas?" she asked. She sounded hurt.

"I thought I should dress more somberly since it's Good Friday."

"Let's not focus on the negative," his mother said brightly. "Remember, He rose again. Now why don't you slip back upstairs and put on that nice little outfit we got you for Christmas?"

Now Roger was glad she'd made him change. Eating all those vegetables with Tiffany had slimmed him down. He looked successful in his navy blazer, like an investment banker.

He smiled down the row at Deena.

She smiled back.

His insides shuddered.

Then the phone rang in Sam's office. Sam was busy making his way up front for the start of worship. Roger eased out of the pew and made his way to Sam's office. He picked up the phone on the fifth ring.

"Hello, this is Harmony Friends Meeting. Can I help you?"

"Uh . . . who's this?" The voice sounded defeated.

"This is Roger Gardner. I'm the pastor's brother. Is there anything I can help you with?"

"Is Sam there?"

"Yes, but he's kind of busy right now. Can I take a message?"

"Please tell him Wayne called and needs to talk with him. Tell him something's happened."

"Will do," Roger said. He walked out of the office. Sam was seated up front behind the pulpit. Bea Majors had begun the organ prelude. It would have to wait.

Roger walked back to the Wilbur Matthews pew and slid in next to Kate Fleming. He hadn't really noticed her before. She looked worried for such a small child. He studied the children closer. They all looked that way. Preoccupied and weighed down.

The phone rang again from Sam's office. Dale Hinshaw was standing near the back of the meetinghouse, overseeing the ushers. He slipped into Sam's office to answer it.

Bea Majors went on with her prelude.

Dale stepped out of the office, looking pale. He walked toward the front, oblivious to everyone around him. He stopped midway down the aisle.

Sam looked up from his chair. "What is it, Dale?"

Bea stopped playing the organ and turned to stare at Dale.

"That phone call." Dale swallowed hard. His chin trembled. "There's been a death."

All across the meeting room, people stiffened in their pews. Deena reached over and drew the Fleming kids to her.

Dale let out a sob. "It's my chickens. They're all dead. That was the missus on the phone. She stayed home to watch them, and she says they just keeled over dead."

"Thank God," Sam said.

"Thank God? Thank God? How can you say that?"

"Dale, I'm sorry about your chickens. But can this keep until after church is over?"

Bea Majors spoke up from the organ. "Sam, would you like me to play something in memory of Dale's chickens? Maybe something from the light classics."

"That won't be necessary."

This place hasn't changed much, Roger thought.

"It's like we're cursed," Dale said. "First Sally got sick. Then Asa and Jessie are having marriage problems. Now my chickens are dead."

"Asa and I are not having marriage problems," Jessie insisted from the eighth pew.

How sad, everyone thought. She can't see what is perfectly clear to everyone else in town. Poor Jessie.

After the service they all trouped downstairs for cookies and coffee. People clustered around Dale, consoling him.

"It was a fine ministry while it lasted," Miriam Hodge told him. "There's no telling how many lives it changed."

"I'd like to think that somewhere right now a little pagan boy or girl is cracking

297

open an egg and finding the Lord," Dale said.

Asa patted him on the back. "You know, Dale, if Good Friday teaches us anything, it's that something good can come from something bad."

"I'm bearing that in mind."

Roger slipped up to Sam. "Hey, brother, you got a phone call from some guy named Wayne. He wants you to call him. He said something's happened."

Sam looked stricken. "When did he call?"

"Just before church started. I didn't want to bother you with it then."

Sam set down his coffee and cookie and hurried upstairs to his office. As he ran up the stairs, he prayed, Lord, don't let it be that. Please don't let it be that.

He stepped into the office and closed the door behind him. He paused to pray again, then dialed the hospital number. "I'd like the room of Sally Fleming," he told the hospital operator.

"I'll transfer you."

He listened as the phone rang once, then again and again. Finally, someone picked it up. "Yeah." The voice was choked and weary and sounded far away.

"Wayne. Is that you? This is Sam. What's happened?"

"Oh, Sam, she's . . . she's . . ."

Sam heard crying, then a click, and the line went dead. He sat at his desk for a moment, thinking, his heart racing. Then he walked to the door and opened it. Roger and Barbara and the boys were standing in the entryway.

"What's going on, honey?" Barbara asked.

"I'm not sure. Wayne could barely talk. I think maybe I ought to head up to the city to see him."

"I'll go with you." She turned to Roger. "Rog, can you take the boys home and get them to bed?"

"You bet."

Their car was parked outside at the curb. Barbara said, "It's been a long day for you. Why don't you let me drive, and you get some shut-eye? Something tells me you're going to need the rest."

They talked for twenty minutes until the hum of the highway lulled Sam to sleep. Barbara drove on toward the city, an occasional truck hurtling past in the opposite direction. Across the fields she could see the lights of farmhouses.

She tried to imagine herself in Sally's place. Lying in a hospital bed, away from her children, bad sick, maybe even dead by now.

Lord, she prayed, if you've ever had a mind to heal someone, let it be Sally and let it be now.

Twenty-Five

A Reason to Hope

What a year this has been, Sam thought as he sat in the meetinghouse on Easter morning.

He and Barbara had spent Friday night and a good bit of Saturday at the hospital, sitting with Wayne and Sally. Sam hadn't had time to write a sermon so he had Frank the secretary remove the word "sermon" from the bulletin and put in the word "meditation." The difference between a sermon and a meditation being about fifteen minutes.

The meetinghouse was full. The men were wearing ties, and the women had orchids pinned to their dresses. Bea Majors played the prelude, and they sang the first hymn, "Christ the Lord Is Risen Today." Sam could hear Miriam Hodge singing the "Alleluia" part, her soprano voice rising above the others and hanging in the pitched corners of the old meeting room.

Then they sat in Quaker silence, contemplating the mystery of the Resurrection. Sam tried to remember how many Easter mornings he'd spent in the meetinghouse.

Thirty-nine years minus the twelve years he had pastored in the next state over equaled twenty-seven Easters at Harmony Friends Meeting.

Twenty-seven Easter mornings in this very room, he marveled. The most memorable service was in 1976, when the elders of the meeting got it in their heads that the youth of the church should put on an Easter sunrise service. It had been Sam's job to say "Behold, the Son has risen," then raise the window blind just as the sun cleared Kivett's Five and Dime and shone into the meeting room. He'd practiced raising and lowering the blind the day before. A sharp tug downward on the string, holding onto the blind as it recoiled.

But on Easter morning, when Sam announced "Behold, the Son has risen," he tugged the string a little too hard, the bracket holding the blind came loose from the wall, and the blind fell, conking Mrs. Dale Hinshaw squarely on the head. Fortunately Mrs. Dale Hinshaw used a lot of hair spray, so the blind took a bounce and hit the floor.

The next year the elders went back to having Pastor Taylor conduct the Easter service.

After ten minutes of silence, Sam rose to

give his meditation. He talked about the Resurrection — how, when things seemed hopeless and the disciples were despairing, Jesus was raised to life, thereby giving us reason to hope.

He didn't speak long, maybe five minutes. Truth doesn't need elaboration or embellishment; it can stand on its own two legs. All the adornment in the world doesn't make the truth any more true. So Sam kept it short.

Then, under the watchful gaze of Dale Hinshaw, the ushers took the offering and Opal Majors sang "I Know That My Redeemer Liveth," which she does every Easter. Her sister, Bea, accompanies her on the piano but plays too fast. By the third verse, Opal is gasping for air and missing many of the notes. But they let Opal sing anyway because they haven't found a way to stop her, and because they believe no situation is hopeless, not even Opal's singing.

They followed along in their hymnals as she sang:

I know that my Redeemer liveth
And on the Earth again shall stand.
I know eternal life He giveth,
That grace and power are in His hand.

Opal finished the song and took her seat. There was more Quaker silence. Too much silence, some of the people thought.

The children squirmed in the pews, anxious for church to be finished so they could search for Easter eggs. Harvey and Eunice Muldock sat on the left side, five pews back, praying. Eunice prayed that her ham loaf would turn out all right. Harvey prayed that it wouldn't so they could eat at the restaurant in Cartersburg. For the past thirty-eight Easters, Eunice had made ham loaf for Easter because Harvey had lied on their first Easter and told her it was delicious, when it was all he could do to choke it down.

Harvey believes the ham loaf is God's punishment for his lie.

Sam sat behind the pulpit dwelling on Wayne and Sally. He and Barbara had expected to find Sally dead the night of Good Friday, but she had hung on and had even been able to talk with Sam and Barbara a few minutes Saturday afternoon. Sally was just well enough to keep them hoping, but not so well that they could rest easy.

Sam could think of little else Easter morning. Indeed, he was so preoccupied that he almost missed the voice. Occasionally in the past, Sam had had the distinct impression that God was speaking to him. He didn't talk about it for fear people would think he was like certain television preachers whom God seemed to speak to every three minutes and fifteen seconds. But every now and then a still, small voice would press upon his mind so vigorously that it could not be dismissed, and this Easter morning was such a time.

I will give you a miracle, came the voice, so real it seemed the speaker was in the meeting room.

Sam looked up to see who was talking, but everyone had their heads bowed.

I will give you a miracle, the voice repeated.

Then, so as to be perfectly clear, the voice came once more. *I will give you a miracle.*

Sam wasn't sure what to do. What do you say when God has promised you a miracle? He looked at the bulletin in his hand. Frank the secretary had bought a book of religious quotes at a garage sale and had taken to putting quotes on the front cover. This week there was a quote from the Christian mystic Meister Eckhart:

If the only prayer you ever prayed was "thank you," that would be sufficient.

That struck Sam as a fitting response.

305

Thank you, Lord, he prayed. Thank you for becoming real to me again. Thank you for being with Wayne and Sally. Thank you for the miracle. I don't know what it will be, but thank you just the same.

He paused and raised his head. From where he sat he could just see the top of Dale Hinshaw's head. And, uh, thank you for Dale, I guess.

He felt noble, thanking God for Dale and halfway meaning it.

Then the Frieda Hampton Memorial Clock chimed eleven-thirty, and Easter worship was over.

Sam rose from his chair and walked to the back of the meetinghouse, where he shook hands and wished people a Happy Easter. Everyone thanked him for his meditation, even Dale Hinshaw.

"Sometimes it's the short messages that do most good," Dale said. "At least that's the way I felt about my Scripture eggs."

Sam was in a charitable mood. "We'll sure miss your Scripture eggs."

"Well, I tell you, Sam, I've been praying on that. Remember how the Lord killed off the Canaanites to open up the Promised Land? Maybe that's what happened with my chickens. Maybe God killed them off so's I could have my promised land. Maybe the Lord had something bigger in mind for me all along. Maybe He never even wanted me to do the Scripture eggs in the first place."

"Others probably wondered the very same thing."

"I can't wait to see what He has in mind for me to do."

"I can barely stand it myself," Sam said.

They walked outside together. It was a beautiful Easter morning. The daffodils outside the meetinghouse door blazed with yellow, like miniature suns settled to the earth.

I will give you a miracle, Sam remembered.

A wild surge of hope pressed through him.

A miracle! He could scarcely wait.

Twenty-Six

The Hour of Truth

Bea Majors woke up the Wednesday after Easter and took her cat Wiffles for a walk around the block. Wiffles had been obstructed lately, and Bea hoped a walk would get things moving in the right direction. That was her theory, anyway. She was too embarrassed to talk with the veterinarian about it. She'd thought of writing the Reverend Johnny LaCosta and asking him to pray for Wiffles, but decided against it. She'd already written him three letters about Sally Fleming and didn't want to appear greedy for a healing.

Bea and Wiffles passed Sam Gardner, who was walking to the meetinghouse.

"How's Wiffles?" Sam asked. "Still bound up?"

Bea nodded.

"I'll say a prayer for her."

"Thank you, Sam. That's kind of you."

"How's your job at the Coffee Cup? Are you still playing the organ on Italian Night?"

Bea beamed. "Oh, yes. Five to seven

every Wednesday night. It gives me a little mad money."

Sam wondered what Bea Majors, with her rolled-down hosiery and orthopedic shoes, would do with mad money. "Maybe Barbara and I and the boys will come some Wednesday night and hear you play," he offered.

"You might want to come tonight. I'll be making my singing debut tonight."

"Do Vinny and Penny know that?"

"No, I'm going to surprise them. You know the song "That's *Amore*"? Dean Martin sings it. You know the one. I've been practicing it at home, and I think I'm ready to sing it in public. Wanna come hear me?"

"Gee, Bea, I'd love to, but, uh, I'm a little busy tonight."

"That's okay. I was gonna sing it this Sunday in church too. I just love that song. It's so pretty. And doesn't Dean Martin just take your breath away?"

"He's a dreamboat, all right."

Sam had asked the music committee to talk with Bea about her musical selections, but so far they'd refused. Bea's sister, Opal, is in charge of the music committee. When Sam brought it up, she'd said, "You never have liked our family, have you?"

"I hope people enjoy your song tonight at

the Coffee Cup, and I hope Wiffles gets to feeling better. You take care, Bea."

"Bye, bye, Sam."

It was a busy day for Sam. He had several hours of paperwork and a meeting with Frank the secretary. Then he drove to the city to visit Sally Fleming. After the promise of a miracle, he half expected to see her up and walking around, but she wasn't. In fact, she looked worse, so he didn't stay long.

On his way home, he drove past the Coffee Cup as Bea was walking in to play for Italian Night.

It's been a wonderful year for Bea. She retired after thirty-five years at the glove factory in Cartersburg. Now here she is, working in the entertainment industry. Opal has suggested she hire an agent and go on the road.

"Look at that Liberace guy. He started out playing in the church and look where he ended up. All you need is an act, something people will remember. Maybe you could have Wiffles sit on the organ while you play," Opal said.

Bea was halfway considering it. Then Wiffles got sick, which Bea took as a sign from the Lord that she was to stay in Harmony. Plus, if she traveled she might not be able to follow the ministry of the Reverend Johnny LaCosta. She lives for Wednesday nights when she gets home from the Coffee Cup, puts on her house slippers, and settles back in her chair to watch *Jeopardy!* from seven to seven-thirty and then the *Hour of Truth* program from seven-thirty to eight o'clock.

It amazes her what that man can do. The month before he'd had a burden for a tribe in the Congo and had asked his television family for donations so he could go there, maybe start a church, and take them some clothes. Bea went through her closet and sent him three of her dresses, two pairs of shoes, and twenty dollars, plus a note reminding him to put in a good word for Sally Fleming and her leukemia.

This week, the Reverend Johnny LaCosta was telling how the Lord had energized his spirit to send healing power over the airwaves and into people's homes. Bea sat watching, enthralled.

She wishes Sam could be like this. She believes Sam thinks too much, that his fondness for reason prevents the Lord from working through him. It was nice of him to pray for Wiffles, but she wasn't getting her hopes up.

He's no Johnny LaCosta, that's for sure,

she thought, sitting in her chair.

There was a song by the *Hour of Truth* singers, then the Reverend began his ministry of healing.

"The Lord is giving me a name just now. It begins with an *S*. I can't quite make it out. Sandra. No, that's not it. Sally. Yes, that's it. Sally. And Sally is sick. She's very sick. In fact, she's near death. She has an illness. The Lord is showing me that illness. I see an *l*. Sally has lupus. No, that's not right. Lord, show me her illness. I see an *l* and an *e*. It's leukemia. Sally has leukemia."

Bea edged closer to her television. Now the Reverend was sweating and wiping his brow with his prayer cloth.

"Sally has leukemia, but by the power of God she is being healed right now. She is HEALED. Her bone marrow is well. Her blood is being restored. She will LIVE."

Bea could hear the *Hour of Truth* church congregation clapping and shouting "Amen."

She watched as the Reverend raised his hand. "Wait. The Lord is not finished with His mighty works. He's telling me more. Yes, Lord, I'm listening." He squeezed his eyes shut. "Sally has a friend. Yes, there is someone who's been praying for Sally. Her name is Bea."

Bea gasped.

"Her name is Bea, and she's been praying for Sally. Bea has another need, which the Lord has not revealed to me. But her need will be met. God is faithful."

Wiffles! Bea exalted. He must mean Wiffles!

Bea leapt from her chair and ran to the kitchen to the telephone. She called all the women of the Friendly Circle and told them what the Reverend Johnny LaCosta had done for Sally. She phoned the hospital to tell Sally she was healed, but couldn't get through. The switchboard was closed for the night, and Bea punched the wrong number and ended up speaking with a janitor. She told him about Sally and Wiffles.

Then she called her sister, Opal, who was skeptical.

"What do you mean the Lord told him about Sally and her leukemia? You've written him three times about it."

"Yeah, well, what about what he said about Wiffles? How do you explain that? He knew all about Wiffles."

"Did he mention Wiffles by name?"

"Not exactly. But he knew I had another concern."

"Well for Pete's sake, who doesn't have concerns? He's a phony."

"You know, Opal, if I were you, I'd be a

little more careful about mocking a servant of the Lord. In the Old Testament, God killed people for less than that."

Opal laughed. "Johnny LaCosta is the one who ought to be careful."

Bea was so mad she hung up the phone and went upstairs to bed.

Bea woke up the next morning and called Sam at the meetinghouse to tell him that the Reverend Johnny LaCosta had healed Sally.

"Bea, I just saw Sally yesterday, and she looked pretty sick to me," Sam said.

Bea began to weep. "Doesn't anyone believe in miracles anymore?"

"Well, sure, Bea. But that LaCosta character, why, he's a fraud. He's just in it for the money. He preys on poor, desperate people who don't know any better."

Bea didn't say anything, but right then she thought of rewriting her will and leaving out the church.

Sam paused, then said, "Bea, I know you like watching *The Hour of Truth*, but as your pastor I have to tell you it's not good for you to take that stuff so seriously. I bet LaCosta hasn't even been to seminary."

"Jealousy doesn't flatter you, Sam Gardner. You're just upset that God didn't use you to heal Sally. Jealousy, that's all in the world it is."

Then she hung up the phone.

Sam sat at his desk, fuming. Frank the secretary tapped on his door and came in.

"I got a call from Fern Hampton," Frank said. "She said Bea called her last night all excited about Sally getting healed. You don't suppose it's true, do you?"

Sam snorted. "Of course not."

The phone rang in Frank's office. "I better grab that. I called the hospital and left a message for Wayne to call me. That might be him now."

"You did what?" Sam asked.

Frank picked up the phone. "Harmony Friends Meeting. This is Frank. Hey, Wayne. How ya doing?"

"Why did you call Wayne?" Sam yelled from his office.

"Uh, excuse me, Wayne, Sam's asking me something." Frank covered the mouthpiece with his hand. "Sam, what in the world do you want? I'm trying to talk to Wayne here."

"Did you call him to see if Sally was healed?"

"Yes, I did. I didn't see any harm in it. Now are you through throwing your little fit?"

Sam shut his door, hard.

Frank took his hand from the mouth-piece. "Hey, Wayne. Sam just wanted me to tell you hi. So, uh, how are things this morning?"

Wayne was so excited, Frank could barely make out what he was saying.

"What? . . . You're kidding! What are the doctors saying? . . . She's out of bed and walking? When did this happen? . . . What time last night? . . . Oh, my. Wayne, that's wonderful. Are they gonna run some more tests? . . . Of course, you know we'll be praying. . . . Sure, I'll tell Sam. It'll be my pleasure. I'll let all the church know."

Frank hung up the phone.

Well, I'll be, he thought. "Sam! Sam! You'll never believe it."

By noon that day, the news of Sally's healing had spread all over town. Bob Miles at the *Herald* pulled his headline about the death of Dale's chickens and ran a two-inch headline about Sally's healing. Bob wanted to leave himself some wiggle room just in case it wasn't true, so he wrote *Church Claims Supposed Miracle*.

Sam got in his car and drove to the city to the hospital to see for himself. He found Wayne and Sally in her room. Sally was sitting up in bed, smiling. Wayne was sitting behind her, rubbing her back.

She grinned when Sam walked in the room. "Hi, Sam," she said, her voice strong.

Wayne looked dazed. "It happened last night," he said. "I was sitting right there." He pointed to the chair next to the bed. "It was a little before eight o'clock. I had fallen off to sleep and all of a sudden I opened my eyes and there was Sally, sitting on the edge of her bed saying she was hungry." He hugged Sally to him. "Didn't you, honey?"

Sally nodded. "I was lying in bed and my body started tingling all over, and after about five minutes I felt like my old self." She began to cry. Tears were streaming down her face.

"What are the doctors saying?" Sam asked.

"They've been drawing blood and running tests all day," Wayne said. "The only thing they'll tell us right now is that her numbers have taken a turn for the better."

"Well, let's just take it a day at a time," Sam said. "Let's wait and see what tomorrow brings."

Wayne looked at Sam. "No, Sam, it's over. It's finished. Sally's healed. God healed her. Bea called and told us about that faith healer she watches and what he said on TV last night. And that ain't all of it. This past Sunday morning, I was sitting here in my chair and I heard a voice saying I'd see a miracle. That's all the voice said — *You will see a miracle*. It said it three times, just as clear as you're hearing my voice."

Sam reached for a chair to steady himself. Oh, Lord, why would you use Johnny LaCosta? Of all the people you could have used, why did you use him?

"I'm awfully glad for you both," he said.

They talked a while longer, then Sam excused himself and drove back to Harmony. He got home in time for supper, then helped Barbara with the dishes. A little before seven, he kissed his boys good night and walked the three blocks to the meeting-house for the monthly elders meeting.

It was a short meeting. Dale Hinshaw was absent with a head cold, for which Sam silently gave thanks. Miriam Hodge dispensed with the old business and breezed through the new business in record time. Then they talked about Sally's apparent healing, except for Sam who sat in his chair brooding, not paying attention. He heard his name mentioned.

"Huh? What?" he said.

"I was just asking if you could close our meeting with a prayer," Miriam said.

Sam prayed, thanking God for His loving-kindness. He wasn't about to thank God for the Reverend Johnny LaCosta, so he kept quiet about Sally.

He finished praying, and the elders left, except for Miriam. She scooted two chairs down the table toward Sam. It was just the two of them.

"Are you not feeling well?" she asked.

"Oh, I'm feeling fine. Just a little scatter-brained, that's all."

"Did you happen to see Johnny LaCosta last night?"

"I don't make it a habit of watching him."

"I don't either. But Bea has been after me to watch it, so Ellis and I turned it on last night. We were quite surprised to see him mention Sally."

Sam didn't say anything.

"Sam, do you believe she's been healed?"

"Who knows?"

"You went to see her today. I called the meetinghouse, and Frank told me you had gone to be with her and Wayne. How was she?"

"She was . . . she seemed to be doing okay."

"You don't seem too pleased about that."

"I'm reserving judgment. So far we have only the word of a television huckster that she's healed."

"You seem annoyed that she could be healed. What would be wrong with God using Johnny LaCosta to heal Sally?"

Sam sputtered. "First, God didn't use Johnny LaCosta to heal Sally. God doesn't use people like that."

"How do you know?"

"I just know, that's how."

"I think God can use anyone."

"You're entitled to your opinion."

"Sam Gardner, you are a mystery to me."

"How's that?"

"Not six months ago you sat at this very table and told the elders how discouraged you were that God never seemed to do anything. Now it appears He might have done something, and you're mad about it."

"That's not so."

"Forgive my impertinence, but I think it is. And what upsets you more than anything is that God might have used someone you don't care for."

Sam didn't say anything.

"I won't belabor the point," Miriam said. "But if God chose to heal Sally through this television preacher, shouldn't we be grateful? Would you have liked it better if

God hadn't healed her?"

"Of course not."

"Then let's give thanks, Sam. It appears we might have a healing on our hands." She smiled.

Sam smiled back. "I still think he's a bozo."

"So do I. But apparently God uses bozos too."

They laughed.

"Besides, Sam, Johnny LaCosta wasn't the only one praying for Sally. We had this church praying twenty-four hours a day. The Catholics were praying, and the Baptists. Fern and Bea and the Friendly Women and even Dale were praying for her all along. And let's not forget that a lot of doctors were working to make Sally better."

"That's right. It probably wasn't Johnny LaCosta after all."

"We'll never know, Sam, will we?"

"I guess not."

"Which means we shouldn't despise the prayers of any one person, should we?"

Sam didn't say anything.

Miriam gathered up her papers and rose from her chair. "You take care, Sam."

"You do the same, Miriam." He paused. "Thank you."

"You're welcome, Sam."

★ ★ ★

He sat at the folding table in the basement, pondering what Miriam had said. How he'd been discouraged when God didn't seem to be working, then when God did do something it made him mad. It occurred to Sam that he wasn't an easy man to please.

Upstairs, the Frieda Hampton Memorial Clock bonged nine times. He rose from his chair, rinsed his coffee cup out in the kitchen sink, turned off the church lights, and walked down Main Street toward home.

Over at the Legal Grounds, Deena Morrison was turning the sign from *Yes, We're Open* to *Sorry, We're Closed.* She waved through the glass at Sam as he passed. He smiled and waved back.

She cracked open the door. "Have you heard the news about Sally?"

"Yes."

"Isn't God good," Deena said. It was a declaration, not a question.

Sam smiled and nodded his head in agreement.

God is good, he thought. Bewildering, but good.

In addition to writing, Philip Gulley also enjoys the ministry of speaking. If you would like more information, please contact:

David Leonards
3612 North Washington Boulevard
Indianapolis, Indiana 46205-3592
317-926-7566
ieb@prodigy.net

If you would like to correspond directly with Philip Gulley, please send mail to:

Philip Gulley
c/o HarperSanFrancisco
353 Sacramento Street
Suite 500
San Francisco, CA 94111

The employees of Thorndike Press hope you have enjoyed this Large Print book. All our Thorndike and Wheeler Large Print titles are designed for easy reading, and all our books are made to last. Other Thorndike Press Large Print books are available at your library, through selected bookstores, or directly from us.

For information about titles, please call:

(800) 223-1244

or visit our Web site at:

www.gale.com/thorndike
www.gale.com/wheeler

To share your comments, please write:

Publisher
Thorndike Press
295 Kennedy Memorial Drive
Waterville, ME 04901